Petey

Petey

by

BETTY CAVANNA

Illustrated by
BETH and JOE KRUSH

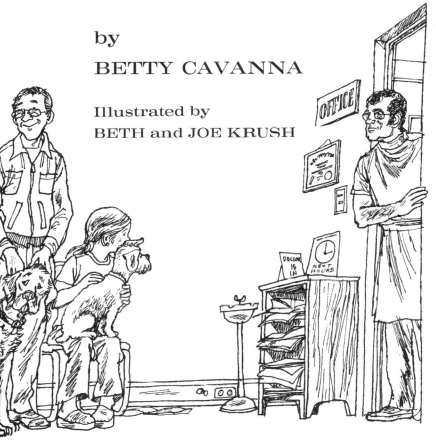

THE WESTMINSTER PRESS
Philadelphia

BOOK DESIGN BY
DOROTHY ALDEN SMITH

Published by The Westminster Press ®
Philadelphia, Pennsylvania

PRINTED IN THE UNITED STATES OF AMERICA

Library of Congress Cataloging in Publication Data

Cavanna, Betty, 1909–
    Petey.

    SUMMARY: A young boy has some unusual adventures with his Great Dane when they move from a farm to a small house in a development.
    [1. Dogs—Stories.   2. Humorous stories]
I. Krush, Beth, illus. II. Krush, Joe, illus.
III. Title.
PZ7.C286Pg   [Fic]   73–4351
ISBN 0–664–32532–7

For Tony, expectantly

Contents

CHAPTER ONE

Introducing Petey

PETEY is my Great Dane.

I should add that Petey is a supercolossal, wide-screen version of a Great Dane. I'm sure that when Uncle Zach gave him to me, he didn't expect a ten-pound puppy to grow so big. Neither did he expect to sell the farm to a development company and have it named Ivy Hill.

To understand why Petey is a problem you have to understand about Ivy Hill. Uncle Zach's big old house—covered with ivy, naturally—is a community center now. It looks like a rooster surrounded by a clutch of broody hens. We live in one of the hens, or semidetached ranch houses, as they're called, although there isn't a ranch within a thousand miles. Except that they're painted different colors, all the houses look alike. They have front lawns as big as special-issue Christmas stamps and back lawns as big as regular eight-centers. Ivy Hill is no place to keep a Great Dane.

Although the farmhouse we left is only half a mile away, Petey arrived at our yellow house on Persimmon Lane in the moving van, along with our furniture. He was too big to get into our little Toyota, and I didn't want to be conspicuous walking him cross-lots. Besides, I thought that if he saw where we were going to live, he might turn around and head back home.

Anyway, when he walked down the plank of the van, he was a sensation. All our Ivy Hill neighbors who had already moved in were struck dumb.

It isn't that Ivy Hill is anticanine. Practically everybody has a dog. But all the dogs are of reasonable size, nicely trained to fit in with a family. There are poodles and cockers and dachshunds, a beagle, a basenji who can't bark, and two terribly stuck-up Russian wolfhounds. They walk past on leashes two or three times a day and stare down the drive at Petey, who cranes his neck over the high wire fence which a handyman put around the backyard.

Petey stares back, wistfully, because this is the first time he has ever been penned up. When he stands and stretches, his tail trails over the fence into the Jamesons' backyard and his head is on a level with the lower branches of an apple tree, left over from the old orchard, which divides our yard from the Browns'. Seen from the back windows of the houses on the next street, he must look scary, but he's mild as a lamb, really. You can take my word for it.

We moved in on the first of March. From the beginning our neighbors criticized my mother for letting me keep such a "mammoth beast" in such a small house. They said things like, "Wouldn't you think people would have better sense?" and "This is clearly a case for the S.P.C.A." They didn't seem to understand that moving Petey to Ivy Hill wasn't exactly our idea.

Let me explain what happened. Uncle Zach is a

beekeeper, and used to send out truckloads of bees to pollinate fruit orchards, but with the small towns spreading into the country, there aren't many orchards left around this part of New England. It was natural for my uncle to sell out when the opportunity came, but my mother didn't expect him to pick up and go to Australia, where he'd heard bees were in great demand. "Give me a year," he had said. "If I think you'd like it there, I'll send for you."

My mother is a strong-minded woman and took a dim view of this idea. She wasn't sure she'd like moving to the other side of the world, even though she hasn't much money and has Petey and me to support. After Uncle Zach left, she raised enough cash to make a down payment on this little house and got a job teaching English at the new high school. I guess you've figured out by now that my father is dead.

Petey adjusted faster than Mom did to living in a house no bigger than a hen coop, perhaps because I spent all my spare time with him. Fortunately, there was a field at the bottom of the hill that had not been built on yet. There was a sign saying that it was reserved for a second housing complex, but I guess the real estate developers had run out of money or something. Anyway, there was a brook at the bottom of the field and no roads yet, just a lot of mud.

"This is *your* field," I told Petey when I took him walking. Then I'd say, "Go, boy!" and he would race along the brook and come back panting and happy. "This is almost as good as the farm and it's all yours," I said when he came back. Even that first day he licked my hand with his rough pink tongue and thanked me with his eyes. Petey understood.

11

Within a month or two, all we had to do was open the gate to his pen and Petey would bound off happily to the field, trotting home an hour later with muddy paws and a contented expression on his face. He never went anywhere else—just down the hill past all the little houses to the field and back. Petey is a very sensible dog in many ways.

Then, in the middle of April, things got complicated. At an Ivy Hill town meeting there was a lot of talk about ecology and inflation, and somehow or other the two got mixed up. Somebody suggested that if the field wasn't to be laid out in house sites this summer, it could be used for vegetable gardens.

This idea went across big. Within a couple of weeks the ecologists, who were against air pollution by machines, found a man with a horse-drawn plow who spent a day or two churning up the mud into uneven furrows. Then he smoothed it down with a harrow, and finally a bunch of neighborhood husbands took over and staked off square patches to be planted in carrots and beets and lettuce and even corn. Petey's playground was ruined!

The only part of the field left unspoiled was a strip of land a few feet wide on either side of the brook, and this was so filled with sumac, elderberry bushes, and cattails that poor Petey could scarcely push his way through. Finally he gave up and sat down, looking at me as if he wanted to cry.

"Now listen, Petey, buck up!" I told him. "It's only for a few months. Next fall and winter you can run down here as much as you like." I tried to sound optimistic, the way Mom does when things are going wrong. Petey, however, wouldn't listen. He had adjusted to Ivy Hill as patiently as any dog on our street, but he'd been a good sport long enough. Now he looked very sad.

Petey has definite moods. After being sad he became annoyed and aggressive. The very next morning he climbed over his wire fence and ran down to the field by himself. They can't do this to me! seemed to be his attitude.

Petey was wrong.

I went down and collected him before I had my breakfast. There were Great Dane paw marks all over the newly planted earth and some labels made from seed packets were trampled flat. I knew that if this sort of thing kept up, we'd both be in trouble.

"See here, Petey," I said sternly, "this won't do. Now, act your age and cut it out."

Petey couldn't understand philosophy. He merely tossed his head and started for home with a defiant lope.

That same afternoon a couple of fellows who live over near the school came up and asked me if I'd like to work a patch of ground on a sharecropper basis. Buzz Jenkins was one of them and Ken Price was the other. It sounded like a pretty good proposition. Invest a dollar in seeds and grow enough vegetables to feed Mom and me for the summer.

"Sure," I said. "I'll go along."

"But you'll have to keep Petey home," warned Buzz, a short, fat boy with carrot-colored hair. "Even on tiptoe he'd be a menace to the things we plant."

I started to get mad. "There's nothing wrong with

Petey. If you're referring to Mr. Brown's tulips—"
There had been a small incident of no importance a
few days before.

"Now, calm down," said Ken, who is skinny and
dark and quieter than Buzz. He acts more like a fresh-
man in high school than an eighth-grader. "Petey's a
fine dog, but he's too large to fit into our garden.
That's all Buzz means."

"O.K. When do we start?"

"Saturday, if it's clear."

Saturday was clear. The sun was bright and the field
looked like a travel poster, dotted with little figures in
red and brown and blue. There were men and women
and boys and girls about our age and even younger, all
busy hoeing, planting seeds and flats of seedlings, and
calling back and forth from plot to plot.

Our section was a pretty good one—not so good as
Mr. Brown's, on the outside edge of the field, but on
fairly level ground near the brook. There were some
big rocks on it, but before the day was over we had
rolled them down to the water and dumped them, prepared the ground for planting, and even patted in two
rows of seeds, one of early garden lettuce and one of
radishes. Three guys all working together can do a lot.

It didn't take me long to realize that my experience
on Uncle Zach's farm would come in handy, because
Ken and Buzz had both moved to Ivy Hill from Boston
and don't know a summer squash from an eggplant. I
guess they must have weighed the advantages of my
country background against the disadvantages of having a dog like Petey around. Well, anyway, I was glad
to be included.

The sun was warm and the work wasn't too hard.

14

Buzz, who has a fat boy's sense of humor, had Ken and me in stitches with his wisecracks. He kept insisting that an elderly couple planting corn in the next plot were putting the kernels in upside down. He almost had Ken believing it, too!

Working together in our garden was great fun until about five o'clock when Petey came bounding over the crest of the hill.

I gave a groan. "Petey, go home!" I yelled.

Petey did not go home. He recognized my voice but didn't interpret the tone correctly. He wagged his tail and took a shortcut across the field toward our plot.

Now, Petey is a splendid sight, with his head held high and his strong muscles working under the smooth skin, especially when he's going anywhere in a hurry. But on that particular Saturday afternoon I was not glad to see him.

Neither were the rest of the Ivy Hill gardeners, especially those in Petey's path. They raised their rakes and hoes and stood waiting like minutemen armed for the onslaught. This attitude did not impress Petey. With an agility surprising in so big a dog, he side-stepped every sideswipe and zigzagged toward me. I felt like cheering, because Petey reached me un-scathed. He put his forepaws firmly on my shoulders and licked my face.

Close behind him marched a platoon of gardeners. Our neighbor Mr. Brown, a thickset man with beetling eyebrows, was in the lead.

"Now, see here, Ernest Bodman!" Mr. Brown looked me straight in the eye, over Petey's protective shoulder, and spoke in a commanding voice. "Something's going to have to be done about that hound."

"Great Dane," I murmured mildly.

"Great Dane, mule, horse, behemoth, anything you like," he shouted, glancing back at his plot along the perimeter of the field and growing red in the face. "Unless he's kept out of these gardens, I'll take it upon myself, as a representative of the residents of Ivy Hill, to call the police!"

Petey put his forepaws down on the ground and backed off rather anxiously. He has never spent a night in jail. Nevertheless, he looked uncomfortable at the rage in Mr. Brown's voice.

"What would you tell them?" I fumbled.

"I'd tell them he's a neighborhood nuisance. I'd tell them there should be a leash law in this community!"

I was afraid of something like that. Petey does not enjoy being walked on the end of a lead. It makes him feel silly.

"Look, Mr. Brown, won't you give Petey another chance?" I asked in a voice that came close to trembling. "He walked very lightly this afternoon, and I'm sure he didn't hurt many seedlings." Petey, sensing that something was wrong, leaned against me lovingly and raised liquid, pleading eyes.

"One more chance, that's all," Mr. Brown sputtered after a few seconds. "One! That's final. Understand?" He turned on his heel and marched away, followed by his cohorts.

"Hey," breathed Buzz, "he sure was sore."

"Yeah," I agreed miserably. "Ivy Hill and Petey don't quite understand each other yet."

While my mother was beating up a cheese soufflé for supper, I told her about the incident. "Mom," I said, "something—"

"Mother," she corrected me, using her English teacher voice.

"Mother, then," I started over with a sigh. I'll bet I'm the only boy in junior high who doesn't call his mother Mom, but I decided this wasn't the time to get into an argument. Instead, I plunged ahead with my story, concluding with, "Petey doesn't mean any harm, but he's always putting his foot in it."

"Both feet." Mother actually grinned. While she's pretty strict about the way I speak and write, she has a comfortable way of not taking most other things too seriously. She poured the soufflé into a steep-sided dish and put it in the oven, then said, "Conciliation seems to be called for. We've got to figure out a way of getting Petey and Ivy Hill to come to terms."

"But how?" I wailed. "Mr. Brown and the others treated him as if he was a saboteur."

"Which he is, in a way." Mother turned to the sink to run water into her mixing bowl, then whirled around and snapped her fingers. "Ernest, do you remember my iris border at the farm?"

How could I forget the iris bed? It was right outside the dining room windows, and in late May the blue and lavender and yellow flowers bloomed on stalks taller than the windowsill. When Petey was a great, gangling pup, he chased a rabbit through that border and knocked half the iris down.

Petey had been in real disgrace. Mom tied him to a tree for a whole afternoon, until Uncle Zach decided to do something pretty clever. "Of course!" I cried, remembering. "The string and the stakes!"

Uncle Zach and I had fastened thin string from stake to stake around the iris bed. The barrier was neither high enough nor heavy enough to keep out a squirrel, let alone a Great Dane, but Petey was a bright pup and Mom was handy with a folded newspaper. "See, Petey," she explained repeatedly, "pretty flowers. No, no!"

The words "pretty flowers" soon began to register on Petey's young brain, and after one memorable set-to he learned that pretty flowers surrounded by string were definitely out of bounds.

"But I can't drive stakes and unwind string around that whole big field!" I complained when I had thought things through. "It would take weeks."

"You can if you have to," said my indomitable mother. "If it's a way to get your dog into the good graces of the neighbors, it would be worth it, wouldn't it?"

Well, for the next fortnight my life was scarcely worth living. I went to see all our vegetable-raising neighbors, explained my plan, and filled a market basket with contributions of twine. The gardeners were generous enough, but to a man they were dubious, and one homecoming husband, seeing me on my knees at the edge of the field, driving stake after stake into the damp ground, shook his head as if he doubted my sanity.

Finally, over the second weekend, Buzz and Ken took pity on me and we cleaned up the job in a jiffy, warning the Ivy Hill planters of the dire consequences of knocking over the stakes or breaking the string. Then I led Petey slowly around the field, letting him sniff the string and the stakes while I repeated, "See, Petey, pretty flowers," until my voice was hoarse.

At last I was ready for the big obedience test. I

stepped over the taut twine and walked along the edge of Mr. Brown's plot to our section, while all the Saturday farmers looked on. "No, Petey," I said once or twice. "No, Petey!" Petey looked disappointed but not puzzled. He stayed where he was.

At this point I asked Buzz to call my dog, then held my breath. Petey's ears pricked for an alarming instant. He opened his mouth and let his tongue hang out, panting to show his anxiety, but he didn't move. After a few minutes he sat back on his haunches, then lay down, looking wistful. Quite spontaneously the watching gardeners put down their tools and clapped.

My big moment had come. I puffed out my chest and preened. Everybody was for Petey except Mr. Brown. He simply mopped his perspiring forehead with a handkerchief and muttered, "It doesn't make sense."

However, the crisis seemed to be over. Week followed early summer week. School closed, to the relief of everybody except parents. Petey continued to behave, and our lettuce shoots came up green and crisp and were promptly eaten by marauding rabbits. Radishes became plump and tender, easy to pull up and pop into your mouth. Peas were almost ready to pick, and carrot tops feathered out in neat rows. Even Mr. Brown's corn cooperated and grew inches overnight.

During all this time Petey never once trespassed on an Ivy Hill truck patch. I trusted him completely, and the other gardeners began to trust him, too, all except Mr. Brown, who had a weather eye out for trouble.

Inevitably, trouble appeared one Sunday morning after church, when Mr. Brown walked down to inspect and admire his greening plot. I came along about the same time, Petey at my side, to find that havoc had been wrought—large havoc! The foot-high corn was trampled and chewed. The beet tops were eaten level with the earth. The Bibb lettuce had disappeared. By now, word had gotten around, and a number of other gardeners were looking on in consternation.

"That—that beast!" Mr. Brown yelled as soon as he saw Petey. "That oversized, good-for-nothing cur!"

Petey is a sensitive dog. He knows when he's insulted. He put his tail between his legs and looked at me to see if I agreed. "Sit," I said. "Stay, Petey." Then, scared silly but trying to look nonchalant and even dignified, I stepped across the string into Mr. McGregor's—oops!—Mr. Brown's garden.

Mr. Brown made a lunge at me, but a gray-haired man named Mr. Mowbry skipped across the twine and held him back. "This is the end!" roared Mr. Brown. "Either that dog goes or I go—to the police!"

"Now, Elmer, control yourself," soothed Mr. Mowbry.

Mr. Brown was in no mood to control himself. His labor was lost, his garden was ruined, and Petey must pay. A number of the other Ivy Hillers were muttering together, and I could see they were swinging over to Mr. Brown's side. Something had to be done—and soon.

Scared, and really sorry for Mr. Brown, I avoided his glare and examined the trampled earth. In a second I was on my knees. "These aren't paw prints," I yelled. "These are hoof marks!" I was glad I had lived on a farm, or I might not have noticed.

The other gardeners inspected the evidence.

"The boy's right," said a total stranger.

20

"And look," said Mr. Mowbry, "here's part of a length of rope."

All the gardeners knew that Petey would have refused to wear a rope. That cleared him. "I'll bet the horse who did the plowing got loose somehow," I suggested.

Several men nodded sagely, and Mr. Brown looked crestfallen, even though his primary interest is ecology. I felt more sorry for him every minute.

"Look," I said, "our garden's in pretty good shape. I'll come over tomorrow and do some work on yours— stake up the corn and replant the lettuce and all. And until your lettuce is grown again you can pick some of ours."

The friendly gesture paid off. Mr. Brown's expression softened and the other faces surrounding me beamed. In no time the atmosphere had changed and Petey was in favor again. Now, if he didn't go berserk after a groundhog and forget all he had learned, everything would be all right, because that same night Mr. Brown brought Petey a bone in apology.

Imagine—Mr. Brown bringing Petey a bone!

CHAPTER TWO

Petey's Parade

IF IT HADN'T BEEN that I needed three bucks to buy a box of candy for Mom's birthday, I'd never have rented Petey out. It was completely impossible to know in advance how he would feel about a baby parade. He's gentle enough, but he gets notions, and when a Great Dane as big as Petey gets notions, there's no telling what may happen.

That's what I tried to tell Mrs. Jameson from next door when she first got the idea that Petey would look cute hitched to the garden cart that was going to pull her three-year-old Totsy in a baby parade.

"This is a very special baby parade to raise money for the Day Care Center," Mrs. Jameson explained in a clubwoman tone of voice. "It's going to be held next Saturday afternoon down on the athletic field. Children from one to four will be entered, and there will be prizes for the prettiest baby and the most original cart." She paused for breath and her bosom heaved. Mrs. Jameson is built in a way my mother refers to as "ample."

"So you want Petey to get into the act?"

"That's right. I think Petey would love it!" Mrs. Jameson smiled.

"I'm not at all sure Petey would love it," I said.

I got up and backed toward the door. "No, I'm not at all sure," I repeated, and I wasn't. But I could see that Mrs. Jameson had her heart set on hitching Petey to that garden cart, and I wasn't exactly surprised when she stopped me before I could get my hand on the knob.

"Look, Ernest," she said, "suppose I suggested renting Petey from you?"

"Well, now," I admitted, "that's different." I had my mind on a special two-pound box of chocolates I'd seen in the drugstore. Because of a memory of lavender ribbon and gold letters spelling out "To My Mother," I came back and sat down on the window seat again. "Petey likes to pick up an odd job now and then. How long would the parade take?"

Mrs. Jameson shrugged thoughtfully. "An hour or so."

"And there'd need to be some preliminary practice?"

"Well—"

"Say an hour of practice and two hours of parade. Petey's charge would be—" I was thinking fast, "would be a dollar an hour."

"Three dollars!" Mrs. Jameson wailed. "Ernest Bodman, that's highway robbery and you know it. You ought to be ashamed of yourself! What would your mother say?"

I kept cool. "This has nothing to do with my mother," I argued, rather untruthfully. "This is strictly a business proposition—between Petey and you."

Mrs. Jameson snorted, but I could see she was weakening. "The fee to be paid after the parade?" she asked in a very businesslike manner.

I shook my head. "Half before, half after." Petey gets notions, you know.

I stuck out my hand to seal the bargain, and Mrs. Jameson took it distastefully, as if it were a cold fish. Meanwhile, Totsy's older brother, Bunny, a little kid in fifth grade, stood in the doorway listening. "You're a shyster," he hissed as I brushed past. I couldn't sock him, because he's a lot smaller than I am, and besides, his mother was present, but I sure wanted to. He's always making these snide remarks.

Outside, Petey was sitting up on his haunches, waiting. He got up when he saw me and wagged his tail. I slid one arm around his neck and said, "Whaddaya-think, Petey, you're in business." But my words apparently did not sink into Petey's canine skull until much, much later.

On Tuesday I stopped by to arrange with Mrs. Jameson for a rehearsal. "Let's make it Friday," she suggested, "so that Petey won't have time to forget."

"Forget what?" I asked. "I thought you just wanted him to haul a cart." I looked at Mrs. Jameson with grave suspicion. Nevertheless, a bargain is a bargain, and right after lunch on Friday afternoon I arrived at the Jamesons' front door with Petey.

"Come right in!" Mrs. Jameson said, talking to my dog. "I want you to get better acquainted with Totsy."

Why anybody, even Petey, would want to get better acquainted with Totsy Jameson I do not know. Totsy is always either sticky or bawling. When she doesn't get what she wants, she yells, and how that kid can yell!

This afternoon, though, she was taking a breather. Her face was one big smile, and she toddled right up to Petey and poked him in the ribs with a fat fist. Petey took one step backward and looked Totsy over.

"Nice dog!" said Mrs. Jameson without much conviction.

At the place where the Jameson living room joins the dining room, a little yellow garden cart, something like a wheelbarrow, was parked. Against it rested a miniature pitchfork and a big plastic bag full of empty tin cans. Red letters painted on the side of the wagon spelled out "Ecology." I caught on.

Mrs. Jameson looked pleased. "Isn't she a picture?"

I gulped and nodded, looking at the cart rather than at Totsy, while Mrs. Jameson bustled across the room and picked up a weird contraption of rope and straps which she draped around Petey's neck.

"What's that?" I asked.

"A harness," said Mrs. Jameson coolly. "See, Totsy can sit on a stack of old newspapers and hold the reins." Somehow she got Petey between the handles of the garden cart and lifted Totsy into it, along with all the ecology stuff.

Totsy rocked back and forth on her fat little fanny and slapped Petey with the reins. "Giddyup!" she screamed.

Petey looked around at her and didn't budge.

"Giddyup!"

Petey sighed and prepared to lie down.

"Giddyup!"

"Come on, Petey," coaxed Mrs. Jameson, but Petey held his ground.

"That won't work," I announced. "Petey doesn't understand horse talk. He only understands dog talk."

"Well, how do you make him move?" Mrs. Jameson sounded impatient.

"Try, 'Go get it, Petey!' " I suggested.

"Do det it, Petey!" yelled Totsy.

Petey caught on. He moved right off across the room as though he were a bloodhound on a scent.

"Whoa!" yelled Totsy.

"Maybe we'd better practice outside," gasped Mrs. Jameson, eyeing a cabinet holding a collection of china birds.

"It would be better to go right down to the athletic field," I suggested. "Then Petey will really understand what he's supposed to do."

So we loaded Petey, Totsy, the cart, and me into Mrs. Jameson's station wagon. Bunny, for once, wasn't around, which was a considerable relief.

At the field Petey went through his paces again and again, circling the baseball diamond at a brisk trot, stopping periodically on command. It began to look as if he might not mind a baby parade after all. Everything looked rosy, and when we got home, Mrs. Jameson paid me my advance dollar fifty without an argument.

The day of the baby parade was a perfect late-June day, warm and sunny. I'd promised to meet Mrs. Jameson and Totsy inside the field gate at one o'clock. When I got there the place looked like a fairground, with booths decorated with bunting and fond mammas accompanied by little kids in everything from square pants to American Indian suits.

Petey's nose twitched when he heard the din, but I put my hand on his neck and stroked him, and he quieted down.

Then I saw Mrs. Jameson. She was yoo-hooing and beckoning to Petey and me through the crowd. She'd parked Totsy on the lowest step of the grandstand, and she had a hairbrush in her hand. As we got closer, Petey must have mistaken the brush for an instrument of punishment, because he put his tail between his legs.

"There you are!" shrilled Mrs. Jameson. "And here we are! Right on time!" From the grandstand, she picked up a straw sun hat that was an exact duplicate of the one Totsy was wearing.

"Come here, Petey," she said.

Petey inched forward.

"Come on. Good boy!"

It was easy to see what she had in mind. "Hey!" I objected uselessly.

Mrs. Jameson took a pair of scissors out of her pocket and cut two holes in the hat about the size of Petey's ears. "I just thought this morning how cute it would be for Petey to wear a hat," she was murmuring.

"Yah, yah, yah, yah!" yelled Totsy at the top of her lungs, jumping up and down. Petey laid his sensitive ears back and looked troubled.

"Really, Mrs. Jameson, I don't think Petey will like wearing a hat."

She gave me a cold stare. "There was nothing in our oral contract about his *not* wearing a hat."

She had me there. To buy the candy, I needed that

27

other dollar fifty to add to the dollar and a half I already had in my pocket. I put my tongue carefully in my cheek and kept quiet.

Finally everything was arranged. Petey had the straw hat tied under his chin and tilted over his right eye. Totsy was bouncing in the cart, all set to go. All the other babies were in a scraggly line behind the grandstand, and the loudspeaker was blaring a march. There was a short break in the music and then the parade began.

Most of the contestants were carriage babies, pushed by their mothers. However, there was one pony cart and three or four express wagons, all deco-

rated up. Petey and Totsy were about tenth in line, and from what I could see they were more of a novelty than all the rest put together. It isn't often you get a Great Dane into harness!

Because I was practically the only boy around the place, I stood back in the shadow of the grandstand and watched from there. As one baby after another passed the judges, I began to wonder how they'd ever choose a winner. Boys and girls under five all look alike to me—equally fat and foolish.

"Do det it, Petey!" I heard Totsy shout, and Petey moved forward obediently. I relaxed a little.

Then I saw the cat! It was a black, scrawny cat, and

it streaked past me silently, coming from the darkness under the grandstand out onto the sunny turf. I made a lunge for it and missed. With one eye on Petey, I called, "Here, kitty, kitty, kitty!" but to no avail. The cat, quite unaware of Petey, made for the fence on the far side of the field.

Even then everything might have been all right if Totsy had stifled her instinct to show off. "Do det it!" she shrieked again, playing up to the grandstand.

When she shouted I saw Petey's ears go up, and I shut my eyes. After a while I opened them again, and Petey and the yellow cart were a blur in the distance. As I began to focus, I realized they were coming toward me, having swerved to follow a flying black tail. There were screams from the grandstand and a high soprano wail from somewhere behind Petey, who was streaking in and out among the baby carriages as though he were on a slalom course.

There was a sudden collision, an upended carriage, and a grass-stained mother who looked as if she was sliding into first base. From the general confusion emerged first the cat, then Petey, who jumped over the gate under which his quarry had slipped, and finally Totsy, slightly bloody around the nose.

Totsy marched forward screaming at the top of her lungs. I sprinted toward her, but Mrs. Jameson reached her first.

"My darling! My angel baby! Are you hurt?" Without waiting for a reply she fixed me with a baleful eye. "You—you vicious boy!" she hissed.

Me! Imagine!

With great restraint I walked over and retrieved the yellow cart, after making sure that the other mother

30

and child were not seriously damaged. I wheeled the cart back and dusted off the partly obscured "Ecology" which decorated its side. Totsy immediately climbed in. "Oo push me, Mamma!" she demanded.

On that note I left. I figured it wouldn't do much good to point out to Mrs. Jameson that justice was really on my side, and that a dollar fifty was still due Petey if the deal was on the level. I walked past the drugstore window and tried not to look at the box of chocolates.

Next door was the Ivy Hill florist. I went inside and planked my dollar and a half on the counter. "Give me what you can for this," I said. "Something for my mother's birthday."

The florist regarded the money thoughtfully. Then he went to the back of the store and slid aside a panel in the glass case to bring out three red roses.

"Confidentially," I said with a sigh as he counted out the flowers, "aren't women the end?"

CHAPTER THREE

Strong Man Petey!

THE ONLY good thing about a safe and sane Fourth of July is that there are no firecrackers to scare Petey. Otherwise, looking forward to the Fourth wasn't much fun. There'd be no parade in Ivy Hill, because a high school band had not yet been formed. There'd be no fireworks at night, no tennis matches, no Sunday school picnic even, because of something Mom called "a recession fraught with tax problems."

Buzz and Ken and I were watching our garden grow one morning toward the last of June when we got to talking about what to do on the holiday.

"We could have a mutt show—a benefit," proposed Ken, who is always full of ideas.

"A benefit for what?" asked Buzz, yawning.

"For next Fourth of July," I suggested lazily. "It's only a year away."

Later that afternoon, lying under the apple tree at Ken's place, we really got down to business. Petey was cluttering up the driveway, and Heinz, Ken's dog, was pushed against the tree trunk, sleeping, while Buzz's pooch, a mostly airedale, was over sniffing at the flower beds.

Ken began to make a list. "I figure," he said, "that out of the kids who have mutts in Ivy Hill we ought to get about twenty-five entries."

"That's not bad," said Buzz. "Charge 'em a dollar apiece as an entry fee and we'd have twenty-five bucks to work with."

"Why not make it fifty cents? Blue ribbons don't cost much," I suggested.

"Blue ribbons?" frowned Ken. "Who wants blue ribbons? This is a mutt show we're talking about, Ernie. Mutts like something substantial, like dog biscuits. No blue ribbons for them!"

"I'll bet," said Buzz, "that the meatman at the supermarket would contribute prizes."

"We could have awards," Ken planned dreamily, "for the handsomest mutt, the homeliest mutt, the biggest mutt, and the smallest mutt."

"And the muttiest mutt," I added, "so that Heinz could win something for his fifty-seven varieties! You'd like that, wouldn't you, boy?"

Heinz wagged his tail and came over and licked my face.

"We could have obedience tests—simple ones, of course, nothing fancy," Ken continued.

"And a prize for the pooch that can do the most tricks. Hank Jackson'd win that hands down, with that pup of his that looks like a cross between a fox terrier and a Boston bull."

Buzz spat out the piece of grass he was chewing and sat up. "You know," he said, pulling his cowlick, "I think we've really got something here."

When Buzz gets to this point, I always know we're in for it, whatever it may be. He's a born organizer. I turned over on my stomach and put my head on my folded arms and sighed.

"General admission fifty cents. How's that?" Buzz was saying.

"Right on!" Ken replied. "We ought to get a crowd. There won't be anything else to do in Ivy Hill."

"We can print posters and put 'em in the store windows."

"We could even rent out concessions for lemonade to some of the other kids."

"We might make as much as—as much as a hundred dollars!" Buzz's eyes were shining.

"For the benefit of next year's Fourth of July celebration," I reminded him.

"Sure! Sure!"

Petey got up from the driveway and stretched lazily. Then he opened his big mouth and yawned out loud, showing his impressive set of teeth. Ken looked around at him and said to Buzz, "How about Petey and the rest of the thoroughbreds? What could they do?"

Buzz was stuck with a poser. "Let me think."

If Bunny Jameson hadn't come by at that moment, walking his aunt's Pekingese, Buzz might still be thinking. But suddenly he found himself looking right into the face of that objectionable little lapdog. This gave him a great idea.

"I have it!" he said, sitting bolt upright. "Sideshows!"

Ken looked at me and I looked at Ken. Neither of us registered.

"We're not bright like you," I said. "Come on, Buzz, give!"

Buzz, who had a rapt expression on his face, ignored me. "Hi, Bunny!" he called. "C'mere a minute."

Bunny, who thinks Buzz is terrific, grinned and came trotting down the drive, the Peke pitter-pattering behind him.

"Didn't you say your pop has a collection of old circus posters in the attic?" Buzz asked him.

"Yeah." Bunny, who is a homely little kid to my way of thinking, looked pleased and mildly puzzled.

"Still got 'em?"

"Yeah. Why?"

Buzz edged forward. "Bunny," he said, "would you like to get in on a very interesting proposition?"

Bunny may be young and homely, but he's no dope. "What'll it cost?"

Buzz made a spreading gesture with his left hand. "Not a penny, chum, not a penny." Then he told Bunny all about our mutt show and ended up with, "We've been thinking we ought to have some sideshows, and if you can borrow those old posters for us, we'll put you on the committee."

Bunny looked flattered but wary. "What do you mean—sideshows?"

"Like at the circus," explained Buzz, taking a long breath. "That Peke of your aunt's is the one that can walk on her hind legs, isn't she?"

"Yeah," Bunny admitted. "So what?"

"Mrs. Robinson, over on Beech Tree Lane, has a Pom that can turn somersaults. Bill Boyd's pointer can be the sword-swallower. That dog'll eat anything. Jimmy Green's grandmother's cocker spaniel can be the fat lady. She won't even need a costume. And Petey—Petey can be the strong man!"

35

Ken turned practical. "What'll we charge for the sideshows?"

"A dime apiece," decided Buzz. "Anybody will spend a dime for a good laugh."

As Ken and Buzz were expanding the plans, I got to thinking.

Petey is a very big Great Dane, but he is not quite so strong as he looks. I wouldn't want to embarrass Petey before half of Ivy Hill.

"What do you want him to lift?" I asked when there was a break in the conversation.

"Who?" asked Buzz.

"Petey."

"Oh! Hundred-pound weights and dumbbells and things. He can pick 'em up with his teeth."

I shook my head. "Not Petey."

Buzz looked at me in disgust. "Not real ones. Make-believe. We'll saw them out of wood and paint 'em black."

"With '100 lbs.' printed in white on the side," Ken chimed in.

I still felt dubious. "It'll mean a lot of training."

As a matter of fact, the job wasn't as hard as I'd feared. Ken helped me make the wooden dumbbells and the hundred-pound weight, and when we got them painted black they looked like the real McCoy. Petey, instead of being stubborn, was angelic about picking them up. He'd sit and hold them for as long as we liked, wagging his big tail gratefully at the praise he received.

As plans for the mutt show zipped right along, everything seemed almost too good to be true.

The day before the Fourth we really set the stage.

We roped off rings and made a row of dog stalls out of wooden packing boxes. We rigged up Scout tents for the sideshows and plastered Bunny's circus posters all over the place.

The next day Petey and I got down to the school grounds early because I was chairman of the sideshow committee, and I wanted to make sure that everything was O.K. We had soapboxes set up outside the tents for the barkers. I don't mean dogs. I mean boys on my committee who were trained to give come-on spiels. I trained them myself and, if I do say so, they were good. Bunny came along in a little while with Koko, his aunt's Pekingese, under one arm and Mimi, the Pomeranian, under the other. A pair of short net ballet skirts his mother had made for the dogs was slung around his neck. We got the dogs togged out with pompoms over their ears and these pink skirts around their middles and put them through their paces in front of Buzz and Ken, who almost died laughing. I don't go for toy dogs myself, but I'll have to admit those pooches were smart. They acted like old troupers who really enjoyed being the center of attention, and they seemed to understand every word Bunny said.

The only sideshow performer who didn't have a fancy costume was Petey. I'd tried a couple of things on him, but they didn't look right. "What he really needs is a leopard skin," Buzz said, "like Tarzan."

Ken was going by just then with a bunch of pink and purple ribbons in his hand. "There's half of a moth-eaten old leopard coat up in our storeroom," he said thoughtfully. "I could get it in about five minutes."

"That's a great idea," Buzz said, so Ken went home

for the leopard skin and we pinned it over Petey's back with some big safety pins.

"That's not quite the way it's usually worn," said Ken, "but it gives the effect."

Buzz sniffed. "It makes Strong Man Petey smell as if he's been in mothballs for the winter."

"D'you think we'd better skip it?" I asked anxiously.

"No," Buzz replied firmly. "It looks swell."

At about that time half the kids in Ivy Hill started to arrive with their mutts, and Buzz had to collect the fees while Ken and I assigned them to their stalls. Things really began to hum. From where I stood, it looked as if it was going to be a great day!

That was the only time I stood still for the next hour. The judges—the manager of the supermarket, the fire chief, and an Ivy Hill junior high school teacher—all had to be shown to the show-ring and informed of their duties. (Explaining these things to grown-ups is always so much harder than explaining them to kids.) By this time the first class of mutts was being shown, and I thought it was about time to get the barkers started.

Bunny Jameson led off.

"Ladi-e-es and gentlemen!" I heard him call, in a half-soprano, half-bass voice. "Step right this way! Inside this tent we have the famous Toy sisters, Mimi and Koko, the smallest, the daintiest, the most incredible pair of hootchy-kootchy dancers in the United States." He gulped for breath. "Did I say in the United States? Ladi-e-es and gentlemen, in the world!"

I paused in admiration on the way to my own tent. I'd written that speech and I was proud of it.

The rest of the boys were doing all right too. All in all, they were creating quite a din, and onlookers were beginning to wander from the show-ring toward the sideshow tents.

After taking a peek at Petey, who was chained to a stake inside the tent and was sound asleep and snoring, I climbed onto my own soapbox.

"Ladi-e-es, gentlemen, and small fry!" I began. "Have you ever seen a strong man?" A little red-haired kid with some sort of bulky toy under his arm ankled up with his dad. An older couple followed, then another, and a couple of girls from my class at school stopped on their way past and giggled.

"That's right! Step over here!" I shouted. "You may have seen a strong man in a circus, but you've never seen one like the one I have right inside this tent. One hundred and fifty-six pounds stripped, he weighs. Not much, you say?" I avoided the girls' eyes and waggled a finger. "But—" I paused for effect, "this mere boy can lift his own weight. Not in the usual way, ladies and gentlemen, not in the fashion to which you are accustomed, but with his teeth!" I folded my arms and took a deep breath, estimating my crowd. "With his teeth!" I repeated. Then I picked up the old cap that I had at my feet and held it out. "Would you like to see this boy wonder, ladies and gentlemen? Would you pay a dime apiece to have a glimpse of the fellow who can perform this remarkable stunt?"

The coins began to clink inside the hat and a few more laughing spectators sauntered up. I was drawing quite a gallery!

Inside the tent I could hear Petey get up and stretch

and yawn. So could the crowd. There was a ripple of laughter. The cap, half filled, came back to me, and I made ready to open the tent.

"Strong Man Petey Bodman!"

Petey stood exposed in all his leopard-skinned glory. He blinked a little in the sudden sunlight, but otherwise he looked quite a character, presenting a dead pan to the guffaws of the audience. Before him in a row lay the dumbbells and the one-hundred- and two-hundred-pound weights. I leaned over, and pretending great strain, tried to lift the hundred-pound fake, shaking my head and mopping my brow to indicate that it was impossible.

"But Petey, ladies and gentlemen, Petey the Strong Man can do it easily with his teeth!"

I snapped my fingers—the signal Petey had learned to recognize—and obediently he came forward, nuzzling the heavy rope I had knotted through holes in the wooden pyramid until he had it firmly in his mouth. With mild eyes he looked up at me, waiting for the second signal.

"All right, Petey, you show 'em!" I shouted at the top of my lungs.

A sudden, sharp noise cut through my words. With a sinking sensation in the pit of my stomach I recognized the strident ack-ack of a toy machine gun. A second later I saw it—in the hands of the little red-haired boy who had been my first customer.

"Stop that racket!" I yelled, and obediently the child ceased firing. But even then I knew it was too late.

I didn't have to look at Petey. The uncontrollable laughter that shook my audience was enough. Tears of mirth slid down the cheeks of grown women. Men stood holding their stomachs, gasping, "Yo-ho-ho!" Somehow I got my head around to where my strong man, his leopard skin askew, crouched shivering at the rear of the tent.

I could picture it all—the pistol-like popping of the child's gun, the change that swept over Petey in the very act of obeying my signal. I could see him fold his head between his front legs and his tail between his back ones, as he had done last year on the Fourth of July when the first firecracker exploded. I could see him slink like a beaten cur to the farthest corner of his temporary house.

"Ladies and gentlemen," I said wearily. "Even a strong man can be gun-shy."

Late that afternoon, under a sky that promised a summer thunderstorm, Buzz and Ken and I got together and counted the proceeds. They exceeded even Buzz's hopes. We had $101.50 to present to the Town Council for the committee in charge of next Independence Day.

"Boy," sighed Ken happily, "that was some show!"

"We've got one problem left," said practical-minded Buzz, "and that's how to get Petey on his feet and out of the school grounds." He walked over to the tent, where my Great Dane still crouched in abject terror behind his array of spurious weights.

I went in and stroked Petey's head and talked to him persuasively, but it didn't surprise me that he wouldn't budge. "There's only one thing to do," I said, "and that's to take the tent down and leave him exposed to the elements. At the first loud thunderclap he'll head for home!"

41

CHAPTER FOUR

Guard Dog

FOR THE NEXT FEW WEEKS I kept Petey away from all social events in Ivy Hill and hoped life would go smoothly for a while. It would have if two very important things hadn't happened. In the first place there was a spate of robberies. The newspapers in Lexington and Concord had been full of such stories for weeks, but in those towns the houses were larger than in Ivy Hill. No one ever expected the burglars to choose this new little subdivision as a stamping ground.

But within three days, Buzz Jenkins had his new bike stolen from in front of his house and Ken Price's mother lost all her table silver and most of her jewelry while she was spending fifteen minutes at the supermarket. After that everybody began to lock their front and back doors and to look cautiously at any strangers who appeared on the streets.

One stranger did appear the very next day, but since he was just about my age he wasn't under suspicion. Buzz and Ken and I first saw him when we were lugging a basket of carrots up from the field. Petey was with us, walking at my shoulder with dignity and trying not to bump against the basket. While the three of us eyed the new boy, the new boy eyed Petey, peering at him through double-lensed spectacles in a very insolent way.

A lot of people in Ivy Hill used to look at Petey in that manner, but since Mr. Brown was won over and continues to bring him bones, the atmosphere has changed. If you discount the Jamesons, Petey is now quite the pet of Persimmon Lane. That is the reason why this kid's stare upset me even more than it surprised Petey.

Of course, at that time we didn't think of the new boy as the second happening, nor did we even know his name, but Buzz said it was bound to be Percy. As it turned out, he was very nearly right. Can you believe Mortimer Augustus Snaffle III? Mortimer was what some of Mom's friends would call a "perfect little gentleman," and they'd be right. Needless to say, Buzz and Ken and I did not exactly welcome him with open arms.

I'll admit, though, that the new boy had a way with grown-ups. Mortimer, whose family had moved in next door but one to the Jamesons, down where Persimmon Lane turns into Huckleberry Road, was always doing little services, like helping old Mr. Thomas across a bad place in the street or lugging Mrs. Brown's packages from the car to her front steps.

Mortimer was also a talker by nature, and it didn't take more than a day or so for everyone in Ivy Hill to find out that he was the owner of a magnificent collie named Beau Geste, who was at the moment being trained as a guard dog.

This term meant nothing to me, but I couldn't admit

this to Mortimer. "Mom, what's a guard dog?" I asked the moment I got home.

"A dog who is trained to defend his home and his family against intruders. And, please, Ernest, call me Mother, not Mom."

I sighed, with emphasis. "I'll bet even Mortimer Snaffle calls his mother Mom."

"What your friends and acquaintances do is no concern of mine. My standards are my own," said my mother with a lifted eyebrow.

That's what you get for having a parent who is crazy for correct English. "Testing, just testing," I mumbled and went on outside.

Mr. Brown was standing in front of his old Volkswagen bus talking to a man who lived around the corner. In a clear voice pitched to carry he was bemoaning the report of a new robbery and suggesting that Ivy Hill should organize for its own protection. "The police," he said, "are fine men but they're overworked. What we need are guardians on the spot."

This, of course, brought up the subject of Mortimer Snaffle's collie. "There's a trainer in Acton who can take a dog for about three months and guarantee that he will defend his property and his people against attack."

"Against robbery, you mean?"

"That's the general idea."

"You know," said Mr. Brown thoughtfully, "if one dog on each street in Ivy Hill could be trained as a guard dog, we'd have a lot more protection than we have now."

I looked down the drive to where Petey was wearing out his tail by banging it against the back fence, and I could easily tell who would be nominated from Persimmon Lane. Petey was by all odds the biggest dog on the street and he looks—quite incorrectly—the most ferocious.

When I returned my attention to the conversation that obviously I was supposed to overhear, Mr. Brown was saying, "A fine generous boy, Mortimer Snaffle is! Sacrificing his dog for the benefit of the community."

I guess he was, too. In spite of his name and his personality, the simple fact that he had given his dog to a trainer for three months lent Mortimer a certain prestige, even in the eyes of Ken and Buzz and me. He used to quote very impressive passages from the trainer's advertising booklet detailing the guarding techniques any normal, intelligent dog could learn.

It didn't take me long to catch on, but I certainly wasn't going to be bulldozed by either Mortimer or Mr. Brown into making a gallant but empty gesture. Petey was not guard dog material. He was death on squirrels and cats, but he could be cowed by a toy poodle. A thunderstorm reduced him to a mass of quivering jelly and a gunshot found him under the couch, balancing it on his shoulders and rear end, where it rocked crazily until Mom and I could lift it and coax him out.

"Petey really could stand a little training," Mom had admitted breathlessly after this incident, and I was forced to agree.

The very next morning there was an envelope in the mailbox addressed to me. Inside was a printed folder with "Guard Dogs Repel Intruders" on the outside.

In a paragraph listing all the breeds approved for guard dog training, the words "Great Danes" had a ring around them drawn in red crayon. Of course I had no way of proving it, but this technique seemed typical of Mortimer Snaffle, and when I consulted Buzz and Ken they thought so too. Nevertheless, I decided to ignore the whole incident, because in small print on the back page was the cost of the three months' training program. I could see it was much more than Mom could possibly raise.

This was a great relief. It didn't bother me in the least when I heard Mr. Brown telling my mother about the remarkable things they can train dogs to do. "In Africa," he said, "they have dogs on sentry duty and in first aid work. They carry packs and they drag sledges."

"In Africa?" Mom questioned mildly.

"Well, maybe in Alaska then. And over here they protect lumberyards, airplane hangars, museums, and all sorts of places. It's wonderful!"

I didn't need eyes in the back of my head to know that Mr. Brown was casting a significant look toward Petey, who was eating his dinner in the backyard without a thought in his handsome skull of protecting a museum or even a lumberyard.

"Really?" Mom turned and looked toward the rear of the house in a doubtful sort of way. She knew that Petey wouldn't know a robber from a policeman. Petey is bright, but not that kind of bright. He may be unusually large for a Great Dane, but he is more used to being protected by Mom and me than he is to taking the responsibility for protecting someone else, and I felt sure you couldn't change his personality at this late date. At least I did feel sure until Ken went back on me and paid a visit to the training center where Beau

46

Geste, Mortimer's collie, was just finishing his first month's term.

"You know how gentle collies are," said Ken, "and Mortimer says Beau was a tail-wagger and something of a sissy. But now he's learned to snarl at any stranger. He'll be a real soldier before he's through."

"Yeah?" I replied. "Well, Petey's a conscientious objector."

Ken, who ordinarily has a pretty fair sense of humor, didn't laugh. "No kidding, Ernie," he said, "I think they might even make a man out of a dog like Petey."

Well, now, it's one thing to call your own dog chicken, but it's another thing entirely to have your best friend and co-gardener act as if your Great Dane wears lace drawers, so I hauled off and said with some heat, "See here, lay off my dog."

Ken just grinned and said, "Oh, skip it, Ernie. I just don't like to see Petey put down, that's all."

Well of course I don't like to see Petey taking a back seat either. But I still felt sure he wouldn't like being a guard dog, especially if he was expected to take care of every house on the street. And I couldn't help lying awake at night thinking about how much I'd miss Petey if Mr. Brown and our other neighbors chipped in to have him trained. The worst part of it is, dogs can't write home from camp.

Along about this time something happened to put the hex on Petey and me for fair. Totsy Jameson, who has a special liking for choochoos, was down at the station with Bunny one evening when the 5:45 commuter special from Boston was due in.

I was down there too, with Petey, because Mom was having Aunt Clara for dinner and I was elected to meet her and escort her home. Well, somehow Totsy broke away from Bunny and toddled out onto the railroad tracks before anybody could stop her, just as the train came swinging around the curve.

I don't know quite how it happened, because just about then I was trying to fix a broken lace on my sneaker, but for the first time in his life Petey reacted like a hero. Before Bunny or any of the grown-ups could reach Totsy, my dog had grabbed her by her short pants and hauled her back to safety, bumping her hard on the station platform but nevertheless getting her out of the way of the train.

There was a great commotion. The trainmen and the commuters all came over and patted Petey on his head and congratulated him. Then they patted Totsy on her head and congratulated her too. Finally, some wise guy had to say to me, "Young man, you've got the kind of dog here that our community needs. He should be trained as a guard."

Of course, Mr. Brown would come up just then. That was all that was necessary to set the ball rolling over the macadam roads of Ivy Hill.

Every time Petey and I popped our noses out of doors we were greeted by neighbors who had turned into recruiting agents overnight. First they'd tell me what a noble dog Petey was for rescuing the little Jameson girl. When they thought they had me all softened up, they'd start to put on the pressure.

Privately I thought that "once a hero, always a hero" did not hold in Petey's case. Mom agreed with me, but you can't run down your own dog, particularly when your dog is as magnificent a specimen as Petey— healthy, single, and unencumbered. Even I began to think seriously that sending Petey to training camp might be a good idea.

One day when Ken and Buzz and I were working in the garden, pulling up the first of the beets to see if they were big enough to eat, I admitted that Aunt Clara had been so impressed on the evening of Petey's rescue that she had offered Mom a check to cover the cost of sending him to guard dog camp.

"Gee, that's great," said Buzz. "I'll bet Petey could run rings around that Beau of Mortimer Snaffle's."

"I'll bet he could too," said Ken.

"Petey'd be as good as a collie any day of the week," I agreed, although deep in my gut I had my doubts.

That night I took Petey for a long walk and talked the situation over with him. Somehow, when it's dark, you get a different slant on things than in the daytime, and I began to regret my morning enthusiasm. Petey nuzzled my shoulder happily and seemed perfectly content. I couldn't help thinking about how lonely he would be without Mom and me. Three months seemed a very long time, and I decided to give the whole idea up.

But by noon the next day Buzz and Ken had spread it all over Ivy Hill that Petey was going off to training camp, and before I knew it Mom and I were holding an impromptu reception and receiving congratulations from our nearest neighbors. When Mr. Brown heard about it, he rushed right over. "Ernest," he said, "you're doing a brave and a fine thing, a mighty fine thing."

I replied, "You bet!" There's no use pretending you're not a splendid character when you are.

"When does he go?" Mr. Brown asked.

That was a point I had taken great pains to avoid considering and I did think that coming right out with a question like that was very tactless. But I swallowed hard and put off the evil day as long as possible. "I think next Saturday," I muttered.

"Splendid," said Mr. Brown, "splendid! On Saturday afternoon Persimmon Lane will give Petey a party. We'll send him off in style."

"And with an upset stomach," murmured my mother, but luckily Mr. Brown did not hear.

Actually, I was proud that Petey was to have a farewell party, because that is one thing that I'll bet Mortimer Snaffle's collie didn't have.

Friday I gave Petey a bath so that he'd be a nice, clean dog both for the party and for his induction into Herb Cannon's training camp. If you have never given a Great Dane a bath in a small yard like ours, you don't know what work is. First of all, you need two cakes of flea soap, the garden hose, swimming trunks, and hip boots. Then you need a sturdy constitution, a good disposition, and a helper. Buzz was my helper. He squirted the hose while I lathered Petey and begged, "Hold still, good dog," with a steady, soothing rhythm. Buzz and I don't have fleas, but even if we did, we wouldn't have them now—not after giving Petey a bath. I'm sure that we emerged from the fray wetter and cleaner than my Great Dane.

By the time two o'clock Saturday afternoon rolled around, Petey and I, both still smelling of Skip-Flea soap, were ready to greet our guests. Mom had made fruit punch and little sandwiches and had fixed a big bunch of flowers for the dining room table. She was prepared for a crowd.

At 2:13 the first guests arrived. Mr. and Mrs. Jameson, who had forgiven Petey's behavior at the baby parade after Totsy's rescue, brought him a pound of hamburg. Mom and I were touched and Petey was appreciative and hungry. He gobbled the meat in two medium-sized mouthfuls and looked around for more. The Jamesons acted astonished. I don't think many people on Persimmon Lane quite realize the capacity of a Great Dane.

Next came Buzz and Ken with a soupbone apiece, then Mr. Brown with a box of dog biscuits, and from that point on I lost track because neighbors arrived so thick and fast. Petey was very calm for a guest of honor. He looked at everyone gratefully with his big gentle eyes and ate everything that was offered to him until his sides began to bulge in a rather alarming way.

I whispered to Mom when I got a chance that I was afraid Petey would either have to park his biscuits somewhere or burst. But she seemed to feel that from there on in Petey was a problem for Mr. Cannon and she shrugged off any responsibility.

About three o'clock, Mom began passing out sandwiches and punch. By that time the living room and the porch were full of people edging respectfully past Petey, and I was beginning to have a hollow feeling in my stomach, because I knew that at four o'clock Mr. Brown would drive us off to training camp in his Volkswagen bus. Petey would stay there and I would have to come home alone.

About this time Mr. and Mrs. Mortimer Snaffle II turned up, accompanied by young Mortimer, who presented Petey with a smallish bone made of green rubber. Now, a collie may like a rubber bone, but Petey

51

would prefer something with meat on it. He sniffed at the thing and walked away, looking disgusted. While Mom was apologizing for Petey's indifference to the present, who should drive up in front of the house but Aunt Clara, who got out of her taxi and came in with what looked like an armful of flowers, but which turned out to be a wreath made of nasturtiums—a lei she called it. Aunt Clara rushed right over to Petey, kissed the air above his snoot, and flung the lei around his neck. Everybody laughed and clapped and Petey looked embarrassed, although he knows as well as I do that you just have to put up with Aunt Clara. What he didn't understand was that she was the benefactor who was putting up the money to send him off to guard dog camp.

In no time at all it was four o'clock and time to leave with Petey. He was still wearing the lei and looked very much like Ferdinand the Bull when we went down the walk together. I think he knew he was about to go somewhere unpleasant, because he had a hangdog expression as I pushed him into the rear of Mr. Brown's bus.

After we got out of sight of the house, I took the lei from around Petey's neck and tossed it under the back seat. Petey wagged his tail twice and seemed to feel slightly better now that the flowers were out of sight. I was glad. I hoped Petey would not live to see another war and be drafted for service in Hawaii.

It isn't very far from Ivy Hill to Mr. Cannon's training kennels, five miles at the most. You turn into a long drive lined with apple trees and after about five hundred yards you begin to hear dogs barking. Some sounded indignant, some furious, and on this particular

Saturday none sounded merry. Petey pricked up his ears and for the first time in his life looked at me with deep suspicion. I stroked his black muzzle and felt like a criminal.

Mr. Brown, meanwhile, was talking cheerfully. He drew up in front of a long, low building from which a big man in a checkered shirt bounded, slamming the door behind him. He wore a professional grin of greeting, shook hands with Mr. Brown, and whistled softly when Petey stepped from the opened door of the bus to the macadam drive.

"Hi, young fellow!" he said to me. "What's your dog's name?"

"Petey," I replied.

"Well, hello there, Petey!" Mr. Cannon looked at him admiringly and stroked his head. "Where's his lead?" he asked.

"He doesn't have a lead," I said. "He has learned to heel without one."

Mr. Cannon looked dubious, but he merely shrugged. "Well, he'll have a new set of rules around here," he said. "When you come back in three months, you won't know your dog. You simply won't know him."

This is what I was afraid of, and although Mr. Cannon flashed a great big smile at me, I felt depressed. "You ought to see," Mr. Cannon was saying to Mr. Brown, "what we've done with the Snaffle collie."

At that moment another car pulled into the drive behind the Volkswagen bus. It stopped with a jerk and backfired, twice.

Petey, who had been standing with dignity beside me, was off like a shot. He raced for a small grove of trees and started burrowing under a garden house with both front paws. Pine needles and earth flew six feet into the air. Within seconds he had a hole almost big enough to crawl into.

This, of course, was exactly what he had in mind, and nothing I could say or do would persuade him that he was behaving like a baby. "Petey," I said, standing over him, "get up! Be a man."

At this point I realized that Mr. Cannon was standing with us, shaking his head in a very negative manner. There was contempt in his voice when he said, "Gun-shy."

"He's afraid of thunderstorms too," I told him.

Mr. Brown looked troubled. "But with training," he asked in a hopeful voice, "couldn't this be corrected?"

Mr. Cannon shook his head more vigorously. "A gun-shy animal," he said, "will never make a guard dog."

"You mean he's rejected?" I couldn't keep my voice from fluttering with hope.

The trainer nodded.

Well, I gave a whoop you could have heard all the way to Ivy Hill, and at this sign of elation Petey raised his dirty face and nuzzled my shoulder. He knew! Somehow he knew that things were all right again.

The drive home seemed very short. While I tried to clean Petey up with two pieces of Kleenex, Mr. Brown kept murmuring comforting words from the front seat. As we reached our door I forgot entirely that Petey was minus his lei and that the people still at our house would be very much surprised to see him back from training camp so quickly.

"Rejected," I shouted to Mom as I raced up the

front walk. Instead of being disturbed, she flashed a great big smile at me and came out to hug first me and then Petey. Aunt Clara dried her eyes and Mortimer Snaffle III sniffed audibly. All the rest of the Ivy Hillers stood around as though they didn't know what to do with their hands, but it was Mr. Brown who really rose to the occasion.

"Never mind," he said to one and all, "regulations are regulations. And even if Petey can't go to training school, he can serve Persimmon Lane by *looking* the part of a guard dog. I'll bet there isn't a thief in Somerset County who would tackle a house in an area patrolled by a pooch as big as that."

At this moment Petey lurched across our postage-stamp lawn, stomach heaving, and in the shelter of the nearest bush he quietly returned all the edible presents he had received.

Petey and the
Little Incident

THE CHANGE that came over Petey as soon as he was made mascot of Persimmon Lane was quite remarkable.

Mrs. Brown suggested this title, and embroidered Petey a red collar with a black M in a blue circle. She barely managed to pin it around Petey's big neck by stretching two large safety pins as far as they would go.

"There," she said, standing back and admiring her handiwork. "You look fine."

Petey is very receptive to compliments. He swelled out his really magnificent chest and strutted up and down our narrow front walk as if he were king of the castle or president of the United States. He looked so self-important that I could tell he needed talking to.

"Look here," I said firmly as soon as we were alone. "You've got to understand you're not a general or a Ph.D., or even a properly graduated guard dog. You've got a new job, that's all. You're just a mascot. A mascot for Persimmon Lane."

But Petey refused to hang his head. The collar he was wearing had made a new dog of him.

I'll admit, in all fairness, that he looked pretty impressive on the evening of his first tour of duty. Mr. Brown had bought a whistle and trained Petey to respond to it. Each time Petey got the signal he would bound through the unlatched screen door and race to Mr. Brown's house. Then the pair of them would march up and down the street in the twilight, Mr. Brown making soothing remarks like "Good dog," and Petey wagging his tail in agreement.

They made a comforting picture together, Petey and Mr. Brown. They both looked sturdy and aggressive. If a stranger had turned into Persimmon Lane, I am sure he would have crossed to the other side of the street at their approach.

But, for a whole week we didn't see a stranger, much less a robber. Mr. Brown eventually grew tired of walking up and down just for the sake of scaring off stray dogs.

"What we need is some action," he said one night when he returned Petey to our house. "He's a smart dog, that's certain. But would he react positively in an emergency? That's what we've got to find out!"

"How?" asked my mother. "We can't provide a burglar on the spur of the moment."

Mr. Brown snapped his fingers. "Why can't we?" he asked. "Mrs. Bodman, you have a wonderful idea. We'll stage a robbery, that's what we'll do! And we'll get the whole street to cooperate."

Forthwith, he called a meeting and suggested that at eleven o'clock the following night everyone should try to be at home and make sure their lights were out. "Pretend it's midnight or even later," he suggested. "Ernie Bodman and I will stage a little incident and make it a night to remember. That I can promise you."

"Wouldn't it be better," I suggested timidly, "to wait until the Snaffle collie graduates from training school? People keep forgetting that Petey is only a mascot, not a real guard dog."

Mr. Brown wouldn't listen to such a suggestion. Like a spirited horse with the bit between his teeth, he kept galloping up and down our living room and yelling that Petey and he would work things out.

I breathed a premature sigh of relief. Maybe I wouldn't have to be part of the incident after all. But Mr. Brown took me aside as soon as the meeting was over and said, "Ernie, you can be the burglar."

"But Petey would never attack me!"

"He won't know it's you," Mr. Brown replied. "That's the beauty of it."

"Frankly, I don't get it," I said.

"Don't you see? That way nobody will get hurt."

"Hurt?" I was still puzzled.

"By Petey. He might bite a real burglar, but he'd never attack you."

I didn't think there was a chance in the world that Petey would attack anything bigger than a cat. As I said before, he's death on cats. All you have to do is say "Sic 'em!" and he's off like a shot, searching in all directions, even if there isn't a cat loose within a mile.

It was this characteristic which Mr. Brown was counting on. He had worked out a really wild plan, which he explained in considerable detail. The house I was to burgle was the Joneses', fourth from the end on Persimmon Lane, right on the curve next door to the

Snaffles'. I was supposed to crawl through an open kitchen window, go upstairs to the front bedroom, and flash a light to signal Mr. Brown that I had arrived.

Mr. Brown would then tell Petey, "Sic 'em!" and point in the direction of the Joneses' house. At the very least, Petey could be expected to charge around the property, barking his head off, and alert a policeman.

"As a climax," Mr. Brown said, planning as he went along, "the policeman will enter the house, capture you, and tie you to a tree in the front yard."

It all sounded pretty silly to me. "A real policeman?" I asked.

"No, Ernie, as I told you before the whole thing will be make-believe."

"Then I'd rather be the policeman than the burglar."

Mr. Brown looked upset. "Ernest," he said, "you are young and agile and Petey won't hurt you. We need you for the burglar."

"Oh, all right," I replied, "but who's going to be the policeman?"

"Mr. Snaffle."

"Mr. Snaffle!" I yelled. "I will not be tied to a tree by Mortimer Snaffle's father. I will not!"

Mr. Brown drew himself up and looked stern. "Can't you forget your personal prejudice for the sake of your community?" he asked. "For Ivy Hill, Ernie? For your mother? For me?"

That is how I happened to pretend to be a burglar. The nearer it got to eleven o'clock the next night, the more I disliked the idea of being tied to a tree by Mr. Snaffle. I suspected that Mortimer's father would dearly love tying me to a tree, especially since it was foggy and raining. Mr. Snaffle knows a few things about the relationship between Mortimer and me. For some strange reason, he seems to side with Mortimer.

About 10:50, Mr. Brown, in a raincoat, an old fishing hat, and galoshes, popped his head in our front door. "Ready, Ernest?" he whispered.

"Yeah," I muttered and glanced at Mom. "I'm as ready as I'll ever be."

A few minutes later, one by one the lights along Persimmon Lane began to go out. I waited two minutes by our electric clock with the luminous dial. Then I opened the front door.

Petey knew that Mr. Brown was waiting outside. I didn't have to invite him to come along. He walked between us through the dark and dripping night, padding softly on his big paws. All I could hear was the shuffle of Mr. Brown's rubber soles on the pavement.

"Have you got Petey?" he hissed.

"Sure." What did he think, that I'd forgotten the lead character?

Mr. Brown strode ahead, blew on his whistle softly, and quick as a flash Petey deserted me for a man he's known for only a few months.

At that moment I disliked Mr. Brown even more heartily than I disliked Mortimer Snaffle. I was left to trudge along through the pitch dark, and all I had to look forward to was climbing through a strange kitchen window in the dead of night and then getting tied to a tree for my pains. As I stumbled along, there was something very lonely about the feeling in the pit of my stomach. With Petey beside me I never felt lonely.

By now there wasn't a light showing in any house on our street. I couldn't see my hand in front of my face and managed to fall over Mrs. Jones's wastebasket, which had been left outside her cellar door. It hurts to bark your shins and the wastebasket wasn't plastic but one of those old-fashioned metal types. Petey should have been here protecting me, I thought, not off gallivanting with Mr. Brown. Suddenly I was mad clear through. This was the nuttiest idea I'd ever heard of and I didn't intend to go along with it.

I scrambled up and wiped off the mud as best I could. Then I put two fingers to my lips and gave the signal Petey has known since he was eight weeks old. It's a bobwhite call with a special trill on the end. Mr. Brown or no Mr. Brown, I knew Petey would come.

A second later Petey's big paws hit the Joneses' drive and almost immediately he began licking my left ear.

"Now you stay with me!" I ordered, and crept along the Joneses' side wall until I reached the kitchen window. "Tonight you're a burglar's mascot, see?"

"Pe-t-ey!" Mr. Brown's voice came from a distance, followed by the sound of his tin whistle. Petey looked around hesitantly but he stayed with me. He understood that I was good and sore.

"This must be the window," I said to Petey. "Yep, here's the stepladder." The window was supposed to be off the latch and I'd been told that the Joneses wouldn't be home. We were using this house for the incident so that no one would be disturbed.

"The idea is this," I said, still talking to keep up my courage. "I go through the kitchen to the hall, walk five paces, and there are the stairs on my left. There's a landing, then they turn. The front bedroom on the right is the one I want. I flash the light in the window. Then Mr. Snaffle comes and captures me." By now I'd completely forgotten Petey's role in the drama about to take place.

I got the window up, although it squeaked a little, and poked my head inside. Everything was so dark that a shiver raced up my spine. "Look, Petey," I said. "If I come back down and give you a hoist, will you come along with me?"

Petey got the idea. When he had his forepaws on the sill, I heaved from behind. It was a struggle but we made it. Petey scrambled inside.

I followed straight ahead to the kitchen door. Bang! My head hit the edge of it. I felt for Petey and together, moving more cautiously, we entered the hall. Five paces—one, two, three, four, five. The stairs should be on the left. Hah! This was a mistake, because the stairs were definitely on the right. The minor error rather pleased me because Mr. Brown always acted like the soul of efficiency, and he had made me repeat my instructions three times. "Come on, Petey," I whispered, "this way."

On tiptoe, in my sneakers, I crept up the stairs, Petey walking beside me as daintily as though he were treading on eggs. No one had told me to be quiet, but somehow, in this silent house, it seemed to be the decent, normal thing to do. We passed the landing and reached the upstairs hall. The front right-hand bedroom door was ajar, but the space beyond it was as dark as a tomb. I was glad I had Petey along.

With one arm outstretched, I crossed the room, feeling for a window shade. Then, holding my flashlight close to the pane, I gave the signal. One flash, one only. On then off. The next second I almost jumped out of my pants. Right behind me a man coughed.

For a moment I froze. Not by the wildest sprinting could Mr. Snaffle possibly have reached the second floor of the Joneses' house in such a short time. This must be the real McCoy, no make-believe business. I'd caught a burglar red-handed, that's what, and I had no instructions on what to do next.

To say that I was scared would be an understatement. I was so terrified that the flashlight fell right out of my left hand. As it hit the floor something brushed my shoulder. With my teeth chattering, I made a lunge like a bad football tackle, and before I knew it I was rolling over and over trying to keep on top of some guy's wiry body.

Petey, the dope, must have been there all the time, but he didn't even bark.

Grunting and gasping, I fought with every bit of strength I possessed. Just as I seemed to be getting the advantage, there was a step in the hall and a man's voice hissed, "Hey there!"

It wasn't Mr. Snaffle. Mr. Snaffle has a high, piping voice, so there had to be two of them.

"Sic 'em, Petey!" I shouted. It was my only chance. I had my hands full already, even if my knee was on the guy's throat so that he could hardly breathe, let alone talk. "Sic 'em, Petey," I shouted again. Would that timid Great Dane go for the guy or would he simply sit and let his master be killed in cold blood?

"Hey! Stop! Wait a minute." There was a tearing of cloth, a growl, running feet, and the noise of a door slamming. Then I could hear Petey barking his head off in the distance, and someone seemed to be trying to climb a tree right outside.

I took my knee off my opponent's neck and he struggled feebly. Petey's barking was mingled with the sound of a voice calling, "Ernest! Ernest Bodman!" This time it was Mr. Snaffle.

"Come on up here, Mr. Snaffle. I've got him!" I yelled, trying not to sound too heroic.

"Got whom? Ernest, what on earth is going on here?" I blinked in the sudden glare of the electric light and looked down on the intruder I had pinned to the floor. It was Mortimer Snaffle III.

"Are you crazy?" Mr. Snaffle was muttering. "What are you doing in my house, anyway?"

"In your house?" I stuttered, getting unsteadily to my feet. "I thought this was the Joneses'."

"The Joneses' house is next door, as you should know perfectly well. Did he hurt you, Mortimer? And what is that beast of yours doing chasing Mr. Brown up a tree?"

As Mr. Snaffle's high-pitched voice rattled on, I came to with a jerk. "Mr. Brown in a tree?" I raced down the steps three at a time. Outside, sure enough there was Petey barking in a ferocious manner, his forepaws high up on the trunk of a Norway maple that had been saved from the bulldozers. In the branches above him, clinging to the slippery wet bark, was Mr. Brown.

Quite a crowd had beaten me to the scene. There were Buzz and Ken, the Jamesons, and the one cop permanently assigned to Ivy Hill. Buzz was yelling, "Down, Petey!" in a hysterical kind of way.

By this time the Snaffles' porch light had been

turned on and Mr. Brown spotted me at once. "Ernest
Bodman," he shouted in a very angry manner, "call off
your dog!"

"Here, Petey," I said.

Petey came at once, laid his big head on my shoulder, and licked my face while Mr. Brown, grunting and

groaning, scrambled down through the wet leafy branches.

"Don't you know Mr. Brown, Petey?" I asked. "He's your friend. But where is the other burglar?"

"Other burglar?" screamed Mr. Brown, pulling his hair with both hands. "Are you crazy? You get into the wrong house and I find it out because I just happen to see your signal. I come to set you straight and you —you—" he spluttered, "sic your dog on me. Now you start cackling about another burglar. Are you crazy?"

This was the second time tonight I had been asked this question, which I consider something of an insult. "I'm going home," I said with what dignity I could muster. I turned on my heel and walked up the street toward my own house.

"And you can take your dog with you," shouted Mr. Brown without any dignity at all. "As a mascot, he's through!"

When Petey and I reached home, Mom had gone to bed, which was just as well. I took Petey upstairs with me and closed the door to my room softly. Then I sat down on the bed to pull off my wet sneakers and Petey came over and nuzzled my cheek. Just for a minute I put my arms around his neck the way I used to do when I was younger.

"Never mind, Petey," I said. "That job was just peanuts anyway. There wasn't even a salary attached. Besides, what dog can serve two masters?"

CHAPTER SIX

The Timid Soul

EARLY IN SEPTEMBER, in the same mail with a long, enthusiastic letter from Uncle Zach telling Mom how much he liked Australia, came a pink card printed with the no-nonsense announcement that all dogs in Ivy Hill must be inoculated for rabies the next Saturday afternoon between one and four o'clock. The place to go was a long garage behind the new water department office. The attending physician would be Dr. James Hugger, our local vet. In return for submitting to a quick injection, Petey would be allowed, or rather required, to wear a metal tag on his collar showing that he had been properly inoculated.

Of course it was up to me to take Petey. Mom's Saturdays were always crowded with all the things she had been unable to do during the week, when she was teaching.

Since it was a rule that all dogs must be on leash, I took a piece of clothesline along and fastened it to Petey's collar at the last minute. Then we joined a long line of dogs and owners and waited our turn.

Every conceivable kind of mutt and thoroughbred was ahead of us. There were miniature and standard poodles, Pomeranians, beagles, golden retrievers, four spaniels, the two snooty Russian wolfhounds, but no other Great Danes. Petey was the biggest dog there.

Inside the opened overhead doors a table and several chairs had been set up. I could see a man in a white coat, a woman writing something in a book, and another woman passing out tags. Petey was making friends with a red setter up ahead and didn't seem at all alarmed by the unfamiliar scene.

Nor did most of the dogs, for that matter. They approached Dr. Hugger one by one, showing no fear at all. The small ones were lifted to the table, the large ones were held on a short lead by their owners, and the entire operation was over in a few seconds. Practically every dog who emerged from the garage was wagging his tail.

The setter, accompanied by a long-haired girl about thirteen years old, behaved like a soldier, not even flinching when the needle went in. Petey, for the first time, began to look suspicious, but also he was curious and I think the setter's nonchalance gave him confidence.

As we approached the table, the woman who was writing in the book asked a few questions.

"Name of dog?"

"Petey," I said.

"Breed?"

"Great Dane." As if she couldn't see!

"Distemper injections?"

This stopped me cold.

"Has he had his distemper injections?" she repeated.

"No, I don't think so," I admitted. "You see, we used to live on a farm."

"You may call my office and set up three appointments," said Dr. Hugger as he came toward Petey holding a syringe.

Since the veterinarian approached from the rear, Petey didn't see him. Before he quite realized what was happening, the needle had pierced his flank and been withdrawn. Petey made a mewing noise, but to my great relief he did not yelp.

I walked home, however, saddened and concerned. As Mom says, it is a mistake to try to coerce a dog like Petey, and I did not think that he would want to see the doctor again.

"Why not?" my mother asked. "He was good enough this afternoon."

"That's just it. He'll recognize Dr. Hugger and he'll remember what it's all about."

"Oh, I doubt it," Mom said soothingly. "It won't be the same place, the same situation—"

"It will be the same man, though. And remember it's three distemper injections we're talking about, not one." I could see Petey going once, but I couldn't see him going back after he knew about the consequences.

A law is a law, however, and Mom was adamant. "On the farm, where Petey rarely saw another dog, distemper injections weren't so important," she said, "but in Ivy Hill, where there's a dog in almost every house, they're essential." To save further argument, she went to the phone and set up the appointments herself.

The first appointment was an evening one. "Come anytime between six and eight o'clock," Dr. Hugger's secretary said. Since we usually have dinner at six, Petey and I didn't get to the office until seven, and by that time the long enclosed porch that served as a waiting room was bulging with people and dogs. Most of the dogs were sitting on people's laps, even a big black poodle named Girlie. Since Petey now weighs 157 pounds stripped of collar and name tag, I thought it would be better if he sat on the floor.

There was plenty of room on the floor, because the minute we walked in a space was cleared for Petey and me. A lady with a Chihuahua shrank back along the wall and a girl with a basketful of cocker spaniel puppies covered them up as if she was afraid Petey would want to eat them.

Two elderly men at the other end of the porch were discussing their dogs' symptoms in loud voices. "I've given him nothing but raw beef and tomato juice for three weeks, but he doesn't seem to get any better," one of them said to the other.

Petey understands quite a few words. Beef is one of them. He licked his chops and tugged at his leash, while the space around us on the floor grew larger.

The cocker spaniel puppies were squealing like baby chicks, and I would have enjoyed getting a closer look at them, but I didn't think the girl seemed very friendly. "What are the puppies here for?" I asked as an opener.

"To get their tails cut," said the girl.

"Aren't they awfully little?"

"Four days old."

I hoped Petey understood. It might give him courage. As for me, the whole idea made me squirm. I was glad Petey wasn't a cocker spaniel. At least he hadn't had to go through that!

The diet discussion was still going on at the opposite

end of the sun porch. A gray-haired man was bending the ear of a robust, bald, military-looking gentleman of the type frequently called Colonel. Finally the Colonel could stand it no longer. "When I was a lad," he said in a voice that brooked no retort, "we had Chesapeake Bay retrievers. They were brought up on chicken bones and gravy and leftover cereal and they were all fine, healthy dogs." At that moment the office door opened. Hoisting the wirehaired terrier he was carrying, he got up and stamped inside.

I began to get fidgety. So did Petey. The late summer dusk had almost dissolved into darkness by the time we were invited in.

"Well, well," said Dr. Hugger. "What's this big fellow here for?"

"A distemper injection," I told him softly. I actually felt I should spell it, because Petey was already looking at Dr. Hugger distrustfully. Maybe he recognized him from Saturday afternoon or perhaps the antiseptic atmosphere was vaguely familiar. Anyway, he promptly sat down.

"Ho!" said Dr. Hugger. "How old is he?"

"One and a half. Maybe he's too old for distemper injections?" I asked in a hopeful voice.

"They should have been done when he was a pup," Dr. Hugger said, "because distemper normally attacks young dogs. At the moment, however, there's a lot of it in Ivy Hill. All dogs ought to be inoculated against distemper."

As he spoke he had his back to us, fiddling with his bubbling sterilizer. Then he turned, with a thing that looked like an overgrown hypodermic syringe in his hand, and rounded the table toward Petey. Petey rounded the table in the opposite direction, not hastily but with determination. "Maybe you'd better hold him," Dr. Hugger suggested.

"Here, Petey," I called.

Petey looked at me with contempt and kept his distance. I didn't blame him. He felt betrayed.

"You go that way and I'll go this," the veterinarian proposed. Petey ducked, and for a Great Dane he showed considerable agility in wriggling under the table.

Dr. Hugger shook his head. "It's always easier to work on an animal when he's some distance off the floor. You don't suppose you could persuade him to jump up on the table?"

I looked at the quivering mass of flesh that was Petey and said, "No, I don't. I think that if you're planning to stick that thing in him at all, you'd better do it right now while he's temporarily trapped."

So Dr. Hugger got under the table, too.

I shut my eyes.

But not for long. The veterinarian and Petey emerged in different directions but with equal abruptness. The glass tube feeding the hypodermic needle was empty.

"Got it!" Dr. Hugger cried.

Petey yelped vindictively and ran around the office like crazy. "See you in two weeks," called the veterinarian as he opened the door.

"You may see me," I replied, as Petey launched himself on a quick trip home, "but I'm not sure about my dog."

That second visit, as a matter of fact, was something to work up to. A few days in advance I tried taking

Petey for a walk past the vet's office, just to get him accustomed to the idea. But Petey wouldn't cooperate. The minute we got within a block of the place he lifted his nose, sniffed the air, and ran the other way. As I remarked earlier, it's a mistake to try to coerce a dog like Petey. He is not only temperamentally unsuited to coercion, he's too big.

When I mentioned this to my mother, she said, "Nonsense," which is a very easy word to say but which makes no impression on Petey.

"Do you have anything constructive to suggest?" I asked.

Mom looked at me coldly. "If you haven't the gumption to make Petey behave, I'll take him to the vet's myself."

That was all right with me. I waved good-by to them with my tongue in my cheek and was not surprised to see Petey come home in just about the time it takes to walk around the block.

Mom followed him, fuming. The knee was out of her new pair of pantyhose and she could scarcely speak for exasperation. When she finally got her breath, she called Petey "that brute" and raised her voice as she added, "I'm through!"

"That's the trouble," I tried to explain. "So is Petey."

Although my mother usually has a keen sense of humor, this attempt at a joke didn't strike a spark. As my grandmother used to say, she had her dander up. Sweeping past me without a glance, she went immediately to the telephone, where she dialed the person to whom we usually turned in an emergency—Mr. Brown.

Fortunately she found him at home, and she returned to me with the information that he would drive Petey and me to Dr. Hugger's office.

"When?" I asked.

"Right away," she replied.

The ride was short and uneventful. Petey cowered on the floor of the Volkswagen bus while I murmured soothing nothings into his ear. Mr. Brown pulled up in front of the vet's, but I told him I thought he'd better go up the drive to the side door. "Petey will be pretty heavy for three of us to carry," I explained.

Mr. Brown just laughed. "You go in, Ernie, and wait your turn. When the time comes, we'll manage."

Dr. Hugger laughed, too, when I told him we'd need help getting Petey out of the car, but he wasn't laughing ten minutes later when we finally hauled 157 pounds of dead weight into his office.

"I still think it would have been easier to do it in the car," I said mildly, while Mr. Brown stood huffing and puffing just inside the office door. Dr. Hugger looked from Petey to me and he was so angry that the whites of his eyes were inflamed. "No dog's ever beaten me yet, and no dog ever will," he said between gritted teeth.

With this he turned toward the sterilizer. Petey began to quake and tremble and the floor felt as if we were going through a minor earthquake.

"What I'm worried about," I told Mr. Brown in a whisper, "is will Petey ever trust me again?"

"What I'm worried about," said Mr. Brown, "is getting bitten."

"Oh, Petey never bites people," I said. "Especially not you, Mr. Brown. You're his friend."

76

The words were no sooner out of my mouth than Petey, seeing the advance of Dr. Hugger with his hypodermic and wishing to be anywhere but in his path, turned toward the one hope of liberty, the door, which was being guarded by Mr. Brown.

The bite wasn't a bad one. Mostly there was trouser in Petey's mouth, but you'd have thought Mr. Brown was being killed. While the vet dabbed some iodine on his leg, he howled and yelled, "I'm going home. But first I'm going to the doctor's and I'm going to send you the bill, Ernie Bodman!"

I guess he didn't know I'd already spent all of my month's allowance.

"You really should have done it in the car, doctor," I said as the door slammed behind Mr. Brown. Dr. Hugger didn't reply. He looked almost as upset as I felt and came at Petey with grim determination and a look in his eyes that Petey didn't like.

As Dr. Hugger got closer, Petey started backing away. He backed until he couldn't back any farther because he was against the wall, but right above his head was an opaque glass window.

Petey can be agile for all his weight. With a twist of his body he was on a chair and through the window like a circus dog jumping through a flaming hoop. Out on the porch dogs, people, and glass all scattered as Petey came through. Mr. Brown, who was halfway down the walk, ran as though all the fiends of hell were after him. Petey ran too.

Mr. Brown made for his car and slammed the door, but Petey wasn't interested in further attack. He headed for home. Of course the person left to face the music was me.

"That window," roared Dr. Hugger, "will cost you plenty."

I swallowed hard and didn't say anything, although I wanted to tell him that plenty was not what I had. There were a quarter and three pennies jingling in the pocket of my jeans. That wouldn't go very far toward replacing Mr. Brown's pants and nine square feet of pimpled glass.

I walked home alone, very slowly. By the time I reached our house I had figured that in six months my allowance might reach the total cost of the two mentioned items.

Mother was sitting on the front steps when I got there. She was smiling, so I knew she had not yet seen Mr. Brown.

"Where's Petey?" I gulped.

"Up under the guest room bed." This was a four-poster high enough off the floor to accommodate even a Great Dane under its skirts.

I felt now was as good a time as any to start breaking the news. "Up under the guest room bed," I told her as a start, "is where Dr. Hugger is going to have to get if Petey is going to be given his second distemper injection."

None but the Brave—

IF ROSEMARY BARTEL had moved to Ivy Hill before the first of December, everything would have been all right. Or if Mom had been a few days late in giving me my December allowance, the worst might still have been avoided. As it was, however, everything conspired against me. Petey, who is usually a pal, let me down as he'd never let me down before.

It all started with the fact that for the first time in my life I decided to be forehanded about Christmas. Right after Thanksgiving I began paying attention to the advertising in the evening paper, and I made out two lists. One contained the things I wanted to get and the other the things I wanted to give. The first list was easy. I wrote it off in a hurry and gave it to Mom without any corrections. The second list was harder. It had a column of figures on the right-hand side of the page and had to be revised a good many times. For instance, originally I had a new dog collar down for Petey. When I discovered what leather collars for Great Danes cost, I had to settle for a new currycomb.

Well, by the time I crossed out this and that and decided on a poinsettia plant for Mom instead of the shoulder bag I'd hoped to buy, I finally whittled the list down to where it just squeezed into my December allowance. In order to avoid temptation, I hustled downtown the afternoon I got the five new one-dollar bills in my hand and handed them over to the florist, the dog supply man, and the news dealer who sells those paperback mysteries Uncle Zach likes. Since the book had to reach Australia by Christmas, I sent it off at once from the post office. It was while Petey and I were standing in line in front of the parcel-post window that I got my first squint at Rosemary Bartel.

Now, I am not the type to be taken in by the sort of stuff that has blond curly hair and big blue eyes. Even on television I go strictly for glamorous brunettes, of which there aren't many in Ivy Hill. That's why it was such a surprise to have this girl with a big sheaf of Christmas stamps in her hand turn away from the window and slip me a cautious look.

You can bet Petey and I did a double-quick out of the post office as soon as the clerk collected the dough for mailing Uncle Zach's Christmas present. About half a block away we could still see the red coat this girl had on, and it didn't hurt to hurry because she happened to be going our way.

She was not more than twelve or maybe a young thirteen. Her black hair was as shiny as a spaniel's coat and it hung straight down her back over the shoulders of the red coat.

"Take a good look, Petey," I said. "A chance like this is rare in Ivy Hill." Walking a little faster, I started to whistle, while Petey clumped along happily at my side. We were gaining on the girl, going uphill,

when all of a sudden around the corner from Huckleberry Road who should heave into sight but Mortimer
Snaffle III, heading downtown on his bike. Normally,
taking the route most of us follow, he'd have coasted
across the Gardners' drive and on down the road for
the longest nonpeddle flight in Ivy Hill. But not today!
Today he got one look at the girl in the red coat and
braked to a stop.

While my whistle died in my mouth, he said, "Hi,
Rosemary."

Petey and I were close enough by now to hear her
reply in a silky voice, "Hello, Mort." Mort! Can you
tie that?

The surprise should have stopped us dead in our
tracks, but it didn't. Petey and I kept on coming and I
believe that Mortimer would have let us walk right by
without any introduction if Petey hadn't padded up
behind Rosemary to take a sniff at her coat and if
Rosemary hadn't turned and cried, "Oh!" in a startled
tone.

"Hello, Mortimer," I said friendly-like, which is not
the way I feel toward him. "Here, Petey," I added,
looking right into the girl's deep violet eyes. "He
won't bite."

There was nothing for Mortimer to do but say,
"Rosemary, this is Ernie Bodman." That he said it
grudgingly didn't matter to me a bit. All I could see
was the girl, and brother, she was something to cast an
eye on!

"Hi," I said, grinning. "Do you like dogs?"

Rosemary didn't reply directly, but she seemed to
shrink into the red coat. "He's so big," she breathed.

Now, from most women a remark like that would finish me for good. But somehow Rosemary's voice was so soft and feminine I didn't seem to mind.

"Rosemary has moved into the house between ours and the Jamesons'," Mortimer couldn't resist blurting out as he stood there making cow eyes. Anybody could see that he felt this gave him a priority on the new girl's attention.

"Really? How do you stand Mortimer's saxophone?" I asked coolly, without letting any jealousy creep into my voice.

"Oh, I enjoy it. I think he plays very well."

Mortimer looked at her adoringly while I bit my lip and squirmed. Score one for the opposition. But I was to get my inning. Rosemary was going my way and Mortimer was headed downtown.

"I'll walk on home with you," I said.

I let it out casually, but I could feel the heat of Mortimer's glare all the way through my skin. Stroking Petey's head, I kept my eyes lowered, because I knew if I looked up, I'd break into a grin. Score one for our side, I said to myself.

So while Mortimer pedaled off furiously in the opposite direction, Rosemary and I walked on up the hill with Petey trailing behind us. Every once in a while she'd look around, and if he seemed to be getting too close, she'd walk a little faster.

"Petey's a big softy," I tried to explain. "He wouldn't take candy from a baby. You'll like him when you get to know him, honest you will."

Rosemary shook her head doubtfully. "I don't know," she said. "He's so perfectly enormous."

Instead of being annoyed at the sincere alarm in her

eyes, I was captivated. They say the first time you fall, you fall hard, and I sure fell like a ton of bricks. I didn't say anything to Mom, or even to Ken or Buzz, because they would have kidded the ears off me. But I began systematically trying to cut Mortimer out with Rosemary Bartel.

There's no doubt that in owning Petey I had two strikes against me. Rosemary was definitely frightened of Petey and nothing I could say would convince her that he was harmless and kindhearted. She always came back with, "But he's so big!"

Mortimer had the edge on me, too, because Rosemary lived between him and Bunny Jameson and because he had known her first. It didn't take a private eye to find out that in the following two weeks he took her to the school play, the basketball game, and a junior high shindig at the youth center. All this in the name of neighborliness, I suppose. Well, I think neighborliness can be carried too far.

One day when I was downtown getting some toothpaste and aspirin for Mom, who should I see looking at those fancy perfumes older girls like but Mortimer Snaffle III. He was on the other side of the drugstore so absorbed in making a choice that he didn't see me at all. When I walked up behind him and said, "I think lily of the valley would suit you best," he whirled around and tried to mow me down with a glare.

Then he turned back to the salesclerk, red as a beet, and muttered, "It's for a girl."

I walked off calmly, having learned what I wanted to know. The perfume cost five bucks with a fifteen-cent tax. So that was how much he thought of Rosemary Bartel.

From that minute on I had one increasing purpose—to give Rosemary a better Christmas present than Mortimer Snaffle. But I was blocked by the fact that I'd long since spent every nickel of my December allowance in a spurt of Yuletide generosity. Naturally, I racked my brain for some way to make a little money. New England had not yet seen a flake of snow, so there were no walks to shovel. The supermarket had taken on its quota of extra baggers for the holidays, and I was too old to stand around beside the wrapping counters on Saturday mornings hoping to pick up a quarter or so in tips for carrying packages. What I needed was folding money! Rosemary Bartel is strictly not a small change girl.

Finally, in desperation, I touched Mom for an advance on my January allowance, but she turned me down flat. It was against her principles, she was explaining at some length, when Mrs. Jameson phoned.

While I sat slumped in a chair contemplating the fact that Christmas was now only a week off and the pockets of my corduroy pants were still unlined with the wampum to do right by Rosemary, Mom turned from the telephone and said, "Ernest, would you like to do Mrs. Jameson a favor?"

I said, "What is it?" instead of obeying my impulse to say no right off.

"It's Bunny's birthday and his parents have promised to take him to town for dinner and the movies. Now, at the last minute, the baby-sitter can't come and they need someone to stay with Totsy."

"With Totsy!" I yelled. "Say, who does Mrs. Jameson think—" Suddenly an idea struck me. "What's it worth?"

"Don't be mercenary, Ernest," said Mom, with her hand over the mouthpiece. "I don't know, the usual rate, seventy-five cents an hour or so." She waved her free hand vaguely.

Dinner and the movies. Three, four, maybe five hours. "Tell her yes," I said, as I did some rapid figuring in my head.

Maybe she'd pay a dollar an hour even. I didn't know what the current rate for baby-sitting was, but even a couple of bucks doesn't look like peanuts when a guy is as broke as I was at that minute.

Nevertheless, I insisted on setting some ground rules. I got Mrs. Jameson to promise that I could come in the back way and keep the shades drawn, and I got Bunny to swear on his word of honor not to breathe a word of this favor to the kids at school. Can you imagine how it would look to Rosemary Bartel if she should find out I'd been a baby-sitter in the house next door?

Mom made me up a platter for my dinner because she thought I needed something hot. This was a good idea because it made going to the Jamesons' back door seem logical, as though I were taking Mrs. Jameson a pie or something. I took Petey along for company and within an hour I was comfortably installed in the Jamesons' living room with the shades pulled down all the way. It gave me a queer feeling to think that Rosemary lived in the next house. I could hear the Bartels' television as plain as could be, and if it hadn't been for the walls between the living rooms, maybe I could have reached right out and touched her. Imagine!

I spent quite a long time imagining. After I ate my dinner and got a drink of water in the kitchen, I went upstairs to make sure that Totsy was covered up, the way Mrs. Jameson had told me to do. The blanket had slipped off to one side, so I tucked it in all around, feeling a little silly but glad to have such a soft job.

Then I came downstairs and sat in front of the cold fireplace wishing the Jamesons weren't the sort of people who kept their television in their bedroom. Suddenly, the house seemed awfully lonely and quiet. Girls who are baby-sitters must have a pretty dull time. I'd rather rustle groceries any day.

After I'd flipped through all the new magazines and glanced through Bunny's latest book in the *Black Stallion* series, I just sat and thought. I thought about how I could buy Rosemary a pretty good present even with $3.75, and about how I'd get Mom to wrap it up in that silver-striped paper she bought the other day. I thought about what I'd put on the card. It was eight o'clock the last time I looked at the clock. I guess maybe I fell asleep.

A frenzied pounding on the front door wakened me with a start. Petey was standing in the middle of the floor growling, his back hair up. Through the din and the fog of sleep I could hear a voice that was certainly Rosemary Bartel's crying, "Let me in!" She sounded terrified.

I forgot all about not wanting to be discovered baby-sitting at the Jamesons'. I was across the floor in a flash and had the bolt pulled and the door open. "What's the matter?" I mumbled, as Rosemary practically fell into my arms.

"Oh, Ernie," Rosemary sobbed, white as a sheet and trembling all over. "I was all alone. Somebody came in the kitchen window, I'm sure of it." She clutched my sweater with both hands and looked over her shoulder in terror.

"Burglars?" I'd thought the burglar scare was over in Ivy Hill.

"Maybe. I just don't know."

This was my big chance and I couldn't muff it. "You stay here," I commanded Rosemary. "Come on, Petey!" I ordered.

"Oh, Ernie, no," I heard Rosemary wail. "I can't stay here alone. I'm too frightened."

So was I, but this was no time to admit it. As Petey and I stalked out into the night I tried to think, and think positively. Probably Rosemary had just heard a twig snap against the window, but I knew perfectly well there were no trees at the back of these houses and my heart began to pump like an overloaded washing machine.

My knees were shaking and my mouth was dry when I tiptoed into the Bartels' house. Only the realization that Rosemary, following at my heels, was now frightened for me rather than for herself gave me courage.

There was a light in the living room but none in the dining room or kitchen. "Who's there?" I called loudly but quickly.

There was no reply. "Come on, Petey," I whispered.

Cautiously, I wove past the dining room table and approached the kitchen door. Slowly, I pushed it open. Then, in a blinding flash of pain, something came down on my head.

The next thing I remember was opening my eyes to

find Rosemary standing over me, tears streaming down her face and a wet washcloth loaded with ice in her hand. Mr. and Mrs. Bartel were there, along with Mr. and Mrs. Snaffle and Mortimer. It seemed an awful crowd.

"Hey," I said feebly, "that thing's dripping."

Rosemary smiled a beatific smile. "Oh, Ernie," she breathed. "You were wonderful." Mortimer looked from her to me in disgust. Tentatively I felt my head. There was a bump on it as big as a pullet egg. "What happened?" I asked.

"He hit you," Rosemary said, "but Petey got him."

"Got who?"

"The burglar," said everyone.

"You were so brave," sighed Rosemary, while Mortimer looked a little sick. Then she actually went over and put her arm around Petey's neck. "And so was Petey," she cooed. "Petey was simply great!"

"What happened to the guy?" I asked, trying to sound very casual.

"The police took him away," Mr. Bartel said. "It certainly was lucky you were next door, Ernest."

"By the way," drawled Mortimer, "what were you doing next door?"

I didn't have to answer. Suddenly, in the doorway, there was Mrs. Jameson, popeyed with concern. But the concern was not for me. Mrs. Jameson hurried into the room and gave me a reproving glare.

"Ernest Bodman," she cried, "what do you mean by leaving my baby alone when there are thieves in the neighborhood? If you think that's what I agreed to pay you a dollar an hour for, you're very much mistaken.

Not one penny will you get!" And with a quick, bird-like nod of the head she flounced out of the house.

Everybody looked shocked and aghast. Everybody sided with me—I could see that. Everybody but Mortimer Snaffle.

"Ooh!" he said in a voice that was almost a whistle. "So you've been baby-sitting!" He made it sound as sissified an occupation as possible.

The grown-ups stifled smiles, but Rosemary whirled around on Mortimer and said in a tone that trembled with anger, "Don't you dare call him names, Mortimer Snaffle. Don't you dare! Why, Ernie practically saved my life." She placed the improvised ice bag against my forehead soothingly.

"It's Petey who really deserves the credit," I protested. Even in spite of the throbbing in my head I felt wonderful. It didn't matter about the money for Rosemary's Christmas present. It didn't matter about anything. I could tell by the way Rosemary scolded Mortimer that I had it made.

CHAPTER EIGHT

Petey Goes Patriotic

THE MINUTE Mom called me for dinner I knew something was up. We were having onions with our hamburger. I could smell them. Mom doesn't like onions, and she doesn't cater to my tastes without a good reason.

Petey followed me into the dining room, and Mom didn't open her mouth when he squeezed himself in to lie down between the sideboard and the table. This also was very suspicious. Petey is not allowed in the dining room during mealtime. He makes it too crowded.

Just to clinch the matter, I slipped him the crusts of my second slice of bread. Mom pretended not to notice.

"Well," I sighed, my suspicions confirmed, "what is it you want me to do?"

She looked up with innocent eyes that didn't quite meet mine. "Why, Ernie," she asked, "what do you mean?"

Now, when my mother takes that tack it means she can't even bear to come out with it herself. As dinner wore on, my concern grew. There was apple pie for dessert—my favorite. Finally I couldn't bear it any longer.

"Come on, Mother, you might as well get it over with."

"Well, as a matter of fact," said Mom brightly, still trying to look as though she couldn't imagine what I was talking about, "Miss Fuller stopped me in the corridor today!"

"Who's Miss Fuller?"

"You know, dear. The fifth-grade teacher at Nathaniel Hawthorne," said Mom as though I should know all the grade school teachers in Ivy Hill intimately.

"What does she want with me? I'm in junior high."

"It isn't you, dear. It's Petey."

"Petey?"

"You see, it's this way," Mom said in a rush. "The fifth grade is having a Washington's Birthday celebration, and they want Petey to participate."

"But Petey doesn't have anything to do with George Washington."

"Of course not, dear." My mother laughed nervously. "It's just that they're having Living Pictures."

"Living Pictures?"

"That's right. All the children dress up and get into positions like the models in famous pictures."

I frowned. I still didn't get it.

"Well, one of the pictures is the Currier and Ives print in which Washington is received by the ladies on the bridge at Trenton, when he's on his way to New York to be inaugurated."

"Yeah?" This was getting thicker and thicker.

Mom took a deep breath. "Well, George Washington is riding a horse."

I'm generally pretty quick to catch on, but this really had me stumped. I asked, "What's that got to do with Petey?"

Mom finally gave. "Well, Ernie, you can see it's impossible to get a horse on the Nathaniel Hawthorne School stage, so one bright little boy got the idea of borrowing Petey. Miss Fuller thought it was such a clever notion that she stopped me in the hall to ask permission."

"You tell her no," I said firmly. "Petey will not want to be a horse." Petey raised his head from his paws, looked at me, and wagged his tail. He agreed entirely.

"But, Ernie," Mom replied, "I've already said yes."

I groaned. I might have known it! Another thought hit me. "Who," I asked, looking Mom straight in the eye, "was the bright little boy?"

"Why, it was Bunny Jameson."

"Bunny Jameson?" I yelled. "Bunny Jameson! That—that little twerp! If he thinks he's going to ride Petey, he's crazy! Bunny Jameson!"

My mother drew herself up and turned haughty. "Ernest," she said, "that will be enough. I have already promised Petey to the fifth grade, and if Miss Fuller plans to have Bunny Jameson ride him, that's up to her. Anyway, I can't see why you've taken such a violent dislike to Bunny all of a sudden."

No, Mom couldn't see. It was just one of those things you can't explain to your mother. Right after Christmas vacation, I just happened to be walking home from school with Rosemary Bartel, who still thinks Petey and I are both sort of special. And what does this little brat of a Bunny Jameson do but follow us for two blocks, screaming, "Ernie's got a girl, Ernie's got a gur-rl!"

Well, of course, just to show I was too grown-up to be bothered by this kind of kid stuff, I had to walk home with Rosemary the next afternoon, and Bunny was there, Johnny-on-the-spot, to start yelling all over again.

"Petey doesn't like Bunny Jameson either," I remarked. "Besides, he doesn't like Bunny's dog."

Bunny got a dog for Christmas, a wirehaired terrier, the yippy kind, who flies at Petey every time he sees him, dancing around and biting at his legs. One day during the holidays, Ginger, the terrier, actually took a hunk out of Petey's right foreleg. Since then Petey makes sure he sees Ginger first. He chases him every chance he gets, but he never catches him, because Ginger's so small compared to Petey, that he can always slide under something and get away.

"Ernest," said Mom, "you're being positively childish. You and Petey are going to have to get over these violent dislikes." There was something in her tone of voice that made me sure it would be useless to argue. Petey would be a horse in the Living Pictures whether I liked it or not—or whether he did either.

One thing I did refuse to do, however, and that was to let Bunny practice riding Petey. "Bunny can ride him on Washington's Birthday," I said, "but until then Petey can practice with somebody else."

"Well, you'd better take a look at the picture," said Mom, "so that you'll know what to teach Petey to do."

93

The next day during study period I went to the school library and looked up the book of Currier and Ives prints. Plate 105 it was—not a big colored picture, just a little thing. Washington is sitting on a ladylike white horse who has her left front hoof held delicately up in the air. She has on a fancy bridle and saddle, and she is glancing coyly downward. A lot of women and little girls, in white dresses with puffed sleeves, are standing around holding garlands of roses. They have wreaths of roses around their heads too, and they all look pretty dumb.

Buzz and Ken, still my two best friends in Ivy Hill, came over at the end of the period and wanted to know what was so great about this book. "Petey's going to be a horse," I told them sourly, "in the fifth-grade Living Pictures."

They both guffawed, which is not the way best friends ought to act when your dog is being insulted. They wanted to see the picture, so I had to show it to them.

"Are you going to paint Petey white?" asked Buzz, and they both howled again.

"How about a mane?" asked Kenny, and they fell on each other's necks.

"Can he neigh?" They went into convulsions.

By the middle of the afternoon it was all over school that Petey was going to be a horse, and everybody who saw me in the hall sniggered, not because I am funny but because I am the owner of Petey.

Buzz and Ken turned up as usual on the Saturday morning before Washington's Birthday just to see what was cooking, and I decided they might as well be useful and help me train Petey for his part. Miss Fuller had loaned me the key to the Nathaniel Hawthorne School auditorium, so we took Petey over there on his rope, which he seems to find not quite so insulting as a leash. Ken happened to be holding the other end as we passed the Jamesons', and suddenly Petey put his nose up in the air and sniffed, shivering. At that moment, from behind a juniper bush, out rushed Ginger! Petey barked gruffly and made for him, with Ken holding fast, swept along like a tail on a kite.

"Let go, Ken!" I yelled. "Let go!"

Belatedly, Ken let go, but his impetus was so great that he landed sprawling on the ground. Petey, furious, began galumphing around the Jamesons' back steps, under which Ginger was crouching, out of harm's way yet still able to take furtive nips at Petey's big paws.

"Hey," gasped Ken when he could catch his breath, "maybe Petey is a horse after all!"

Just then Bunny Jameson arrived on the scene, his face streaked with grime, wearing the most irritating grin in the world.

"Petey's a horse!" he screamed. "Petey's a horse! Giddyup, Petey!" Brandishing an imaginary whip, he made for my dog.

Fortunately, I caught him first. "You leave Petey alone," I said sternly. "You'll ride Petey just once, d'you hear, just once, then never again so long as you live!"

Bunny wriggled out of my grasp and backed off, still grinning. "Ernie's got a girl!" he shrieked in falsetto. "Ernie's got a gur-rl!" Then he ran like mad for the next street.

Buzz looked at Ken and Ken looked at Buzz. "Have you, Ernie?" they asked.

My face got red, for no reason except a nervous reaction I have. "Don't pay any attention to that kid," I advised, as I tugged at Petey's rope and started off ahead.

When we got over to the school we posed Petey on the little stage. Ken, who is the smallest of the three of us, sat on his back, while I tried to make Petey hold his left paw in the air like George Washington's horse in the picture.

Petey behaved quite well. He wriggled a little at first, but after he got used to Ken's weight he began to enjoy being the center of attention. When I thought, though, of all those little girls in white dresses kneeling around and looking up adoringly, I began to have qualms. Petey wouldn't know they were looking at George Washington. He might think they were looking at him. That sort of thing often goes to Petey's head. He's apt to roll over like a puppy and want his belly rubbed. In a way I hoped he would—roll over, I mean—if Bunny Jameson was underneath!

On the day of the celebration I was excused from English class to take Petey over to the Nathaniel Hawthorne School half an hour before the Living Pictures were to begin.

There was a rustle of amusement when I got up to go. As I turned to open the door, I saw Ken nudge Buzz. The reason was that Rosemary Bartel had picked up her books and was leaving the room too, and although I ducked out of that door pretty quick, she was right behind me.

I turned and waited.

"Isn't this the day Petey is a horse?" she asked when she caught up.

"How did you hear about that?"

Rosemary smiled. She has a really nice smile that makes her eyes turn up at the corners. "Oh, everybody knows about Petey!" she laughed. "I think it's very funny, and sort of sweet."

"Where are you going?" I asked, mollified.

"Me? I'm going over to help make up the children for the Living Pictures. It's part of my course in dramatic art."

"Oh!" My heart hit the bottom of my stomach.

"It's nice we're both going, isn't it?"

No, I thought. Definitely, no. But that is not one of the things you can say to a girl without being misunderstood. "Look, Rosemary," I said after I swallowed a couple of times, "if Bunny Jameson starts teasing you, ignore him, see?"

Rosemary opened her violet eyes very wide. "But why would Bunny Jameson tease me?"

"I mean, if he says anything about me—anything silly."

"About you?"

"About us, then. About you and me. Just pay no attention."

I left her on the corner of Beechnut Drive. She walked on toward the school while I went home for Petey. I fooled around awhile because I wanted to arrive at Nathaniel Hawthorne School as late as possible. There was no point to taking any chances on Bunny's getting funny in front of all those grade school teachers and making a crack about Rosemary. I figured if I got

Petey there just in time for Bunny to mount him and not a minute before, I'd be pretty safe.

Miss Fuller had sent me a copy of the program. "Washington Crossing the Delaware" came first, then "General Burgoyne's Surrender," then Petey.

When I pushed open the gate of the schoolyard, I could hear some applause coming from the auditorium. That must be Washington in the rowboat, I thought. At that moment Miss Fuller popped her head out the window of the little dressing room next to the stage and looked relieved when she saw Petey.

"Oh, there you are!" she called in a hoarse whisper. "Hurry up, Ernie! The 'Bridge at Trenton' is next."

"O. K.," I replied. "Come on, Petey! On the double!"

As we tiptoed past the door to the auditorium, I could see there was quite a crowd—all the children from the lower grades and a good many mothers of fifth-grade kids who were performing.

"Behave now, Petey!" I warned, as I opened the door of the dressing room. It was jam-packed with a rowboat and teachers and children. I couldn't even see Rosemary in the frantic commotion.

"Oh, there you are!" Miss Fuller said again when she saw me trapped by the throng.

"I don't think I can get Petey in," I said, "until you get some of the army out."

Miss Fuller seemed to agree. She clapped her hands softly. "Washington," she said, "take the men in the boat downstairs. Quietly, now!"

Just then General Burgoyne's defeated soldiers began to pour off the stage, and they made the anteroom even more crowded than before. It took quite a few minutes to get rid of them, while Petey and I struggled with the bridle Miss Fuller tossed at me. Petey did not like that bridle, not one bit. It reminded him of a leash.

I managed to get it hooked up, though, just as Rosemary came over with an old piano throw that was to be Petey's saddle blanket.

"He looks unhappy," she said.

"If you were a dog, wouldn't you be?"

Before Rosemary could reply, Bunny Jameson disentangled himself from the gang of youngsters. He was a very short, squat George Washington, with an enormous cocked hat down over his ears. "Hey! Where's my horse?" he asked as if he were blind.

Rosemary took one dismayed look at him. "What have you done to your eyebrows?"

Bunny pushed back his hat. "Wha'sa matter with my eyebrows?" He rubbed one with a pudgy hand and came away with a palm black with greasepaint.

Rosemary wailed softly. "Come here to me! I'll have to do them all over again." Holding firmly to Bunny's arm, she led him away.

Miss Fuller was rounding up some little girls with roses in their hair. "Come on, now," she was saying in a strained voice. "Take your positions. Hurry up!" Then she looked around. "Where's Bunny?"

"He's right here, Miss Fuller. He smeared his eyebrows. Get the horse in the picture and Bunny can get on last." It didn't quite make sense, what Rosemary was saying, but everybody understood.

"All right, Ernest, bring on the horse."

I led Petey through the dressing room and up the few steps to the stage. My Great Dane looked at the little girls and the roses they were holding. Then he looked anxiously at me.

"Now, Petey, come on," I said persuasively.

Petey sat down.

"What's the matter with him?" snapped Miss Fuller.

"I kept telling everybody all along," I explained, "that Petey wouldn't like being a horse."

"You didn't tell me," said Miss Fuller truthfully. She came over and started to tug at the bridle. Petey looked at her balefully.

"You'd better let me handle him if you want him to be in the picture," I suggested.

"Well, hurry!"

Of course anybody who's even slightly acquainted with him knows that you can't hurry Petey. Still, I did my best, coaxing and encouraging, until reluctantly Petey moved forward toward the bevy of little girls. When he got into position, I arranged him carefully, head down and one paw in the air. "Stay!" I ordered. A light of comprehension seemed to come into his eyes. He'd done something of this sort before.

Miss Fuller peeked through the curtains, then hurried to the dressing room door. "Quick, Rosemary," she called, "the audience is getting restless."

"All right. He's ready."

Bunny, his eyebrows reestablished, scampered onto the stage.

"Get behind scenes, Ernest!" Miss Fuller rapped out orders. "Up you go, Bunny. Hat in your hand. That's right. Fine! Curtain!"

The curtain was pulled back, and from my place in the wings I could see Petey cock his ears and sniff. He

kept his forepaw raised, but he turned his head and deliberately took a good long whiff of Bunny Jameson.

My heart stopped beating. Why hadn't I thought of it before? He smelled Ginger! And with the way Petey hates Ginger!

I took an impulsive step forward, but only one! Before I could take another, Petey, barking at the top of his lungs, had leaped over the bevy of little girls and off the stage. In two or three bounds he was out of the auditorium and racing downstairs, with Bunny lying along his back like a jockey. Unlike a jockey's, however, both of Bunny's arms were around Petey's neck. He was hanging on like grim death and yelling as loud as he could. Between Bunny's screams and Petey's barks you could trace their course the length of Beechnut Drive.

"He'll be killed!" cried Miss Fuller, running to the dressing room window, while half the audience rose as if to follow.

"Not Bunny!" I said.

Rosemary, who had also crowded to the window, was rewarded by a sight of Petey's and Bunny's rear ends, just before they disappeared from view.

"That Petey!" she said, convulsed with laughter. "He's got the Bridge at Trenton mixed up with Paul Revere's Ride!"

Miss Fuller looked at her icily. "That is not funny," she said as she went back to apologize to the startled audience.

Rosemary chuckled again, softly, and looked at me, her eyes twinkling. "Is it true," she asked, "what Bunny says?"

"What did he say?" I could feel the red creeping above the collar of my shirt.

Rosemary lowered her lashes, a trick women have, and looked up at me. "That I am your girl?"

Well, how can a fellow reply to a question like that?

CHAPTER NINE

Fireman's Holiday

TO BEGIN WITH, I didn't want to go to a Memorial Day picnic because I have no love for the Snaffles, old or—most particularly—young. To end with, I wanted to stick around home because holidays are swell days for fires.

But Mom insisted.

"Ernie," she said, "this attitude of yours toward Mortimer is ridiculous. He's a perfectly nice boy, with lovely manners."

"Perfectly nice," I mimicked.

"What did you say?"

"Nothing." There's no use trying to explain to a woman—especially to a mother—that a guy who looks more than a little like that collie of his does not appeal to me, nor to Petey, who began to rub his shoulder against mine in agreement.

"Look," I said, because Petey gave me courage. "While we're off on this picnic, suppose there's a fire?"

"Fire?" Mom looked up from the egg-sized hole in my sock she was trying to darn and murmured, "Fire?"

I tore my hair. I beat my heels on the floor. I groaned, and Petey wagged his tail. "Don't tell me you've forgotten I'm an honorary member of the Ivy Hill Volunteer Fire Company?"

"Oh, that."

For an English teacher who seemed pleased as Punch when I won the junior high school essay contest last month and earned this title, along with the privilege of being allowed to ride along on the truck to all fires occurring through the month of May, my mother was acting dim-witted. "It's not 'Oh, that' at all," I said firmly. "To me, it's doggoned important." At the word "dog" Petey wagged his tail again.

"I'm sure it is, Ernie." Mom sounded mildly apologetic.

"You don't understand a thing about it," I persisted. My feelings were hurt. "Firemen in Ivy Hill do a great public service. Risking their lives—"

"Risking your life?" Mom's voice rose sharply. "Now listen here, Ernest, if that's what it amounts to, you can just resign. Today. I'll call Mr. Talbot myself."

"Mr. Talbot is the school principal," I said patiently. "This is the Fire Company."

"I don't care. You can call the Fire Company. Right away."

Naturally, I couldn't do that. Still, I had to pacify my mother. "I'm not going to get hurt," I promised. "I'm only an honorary member, even though they gave me a badge."

"And just what does that mean?"

"I just get to ride along, that's all."

Mom still looked suspicious, so I tried to be even more soothing. "It'll be just my luck if the whole month goes by without one decent fire," I complained.

Mom bit off her thread and shot me a look. "Ernie, that's a dreadful thing to say!"

"I don't see why it's so dreadful. The Volunteer Fire Company needs practice. How are these guys ever going to learn how to rescue women and children from burning buildings otherwise? That's what I want to know."

"Burning buildings! Ernie, you're not to go anywhere near a burning building. Why, just last week a whole wall collapsed in Boston and buried a truck and six men in the debris. You look right into my eyes and promise me!" Mom sounded all wrought up.

"Promise me this very minute! Or I'll telephone the fire chief myself."

She would too. My mother is very strong-minded. Instead of talking myself out of the Memorial Day picnic, I'd talked myself into a jam. I had to think fast.

"Now, Mother," I said, keeping my voice very calm, "there hasn't been a fire since I won the essay contest, and there probably won't be for ages, and when there is one, it'll probably be just a stinky little grass fire that doesn't amount to a hill of beans."

Mom looked unconvinced but cagey. "So what's all this talk about fires on holidays?"

"Poof," I said lightly. "There won't be a fire. What would start a fire?"

"Then there's no reason," said Mom with an air of finality, "why you shouldn't go on a picnic with the Snaffles and me."

Hitting below the belt, I'd call it. "That," I told Petey as we walked over to Ken's house in the mild May sunshine, "is how a woman always wins."

It helps to have a friend you can talk things over

with, and Ken was very understanding. "That's rotten luck," he agreed when he heard my story. "There's sure to be a fire on Memorial Day." I looked so downcast he suddenly turned hopeful. "Maybe it'll rain," he said.

No such luck. The holiday was perfect, warm and sunny. Mom started deviling eggs and making sandwiches right after breakfast. "You get the hamper down from the storeroom," she ordered carefully. "It's beautiful weather for a picnic!"

"It's not so good for a fire," I replied spitefully. "There ought to be more wind." But Mom was so absorbed in tasting sandwich fillings that she didn't even hear.

The Snaffles arrived about eleven thirty, all three of them wedged into the front seat of their Chevy. Mom bustled out happily, carrying the picnic basket, and I closed the front door and whistled to Petey.

"Oh, Ernie!" Mom cried from the car, "you're not taking Petey!"

There are times when a fellow has to be firm. "Either Petey goes," I said decidedly, "or I stay."

Mom looked daggers at me, but I knew she'd feel that this was no time to start an argument. She couldn't punish me, except to leave me home, and that wouldn't be any punishment. For the first time in my life I won a round. Petey went.

I could tell that this bugged Mortimer, because Beau had been left at home as usual. That's what comes from being a graduate guard dog. You have to stay in the house and guard the place. I was glad Petey had flunked out.

The car seat kind of drooped where he sat, and

Mom and I kept sliding toward him, but otherwise we were as comfortable as could be. Petey is a well-behaved dog. He never raises a ruckus.

We didn't have far to go, anyway. "I thought we'd park along the road and walk back to the stream that runs through the old Clarke property," Mr. Snaffle said. "We handle Mr. Clarke's insurance, and he's always told me that anytime we wanted to picnic there it'd be perfectly all right, especially since there's nobody living there now."

I looked at Mom in real disgust. "Some place for a picnic!" I muttered to Mom under my breath.

"Sh!" She frowned and started talking to Mrs. Snaffle, pointedly ignoring me.

I knew the Clarke property like a book. Permission or no permission, all of us boys had been over every inch of it. There was a piddly little stream of water hardly deep enough to wet your toes in, let alone swim. A fine choice!

Looking very bored, I helped unload the car, and gave Mortimer the biggest basket to carry. Mr. Snaffle himself took charge of a bag of charcoal and a charcoal grill, which was the only bright spot in the picture.

"Mmm. Steaks?" I asked him.

"Steaks, in times like these? Hamburg."

You can see what it gets a guy to look on the bright side of things.

Well, the five of us tramped through a field or two of high grass until we reached the creek. Then we walked up the creek for a few hundred yards until we got to a place where there were a lot of tall trees and sort of a carpet of grass. I'll admit it was pretty. The sun shone through the trees and fell in spots on the ground, and up on the right the old Clarke barn looked like something an artist would choose to paint. But prettiness, at a picnic, isn't enough for me. I've got to do something.

And there wasn't anything to do. No swimming. No fishing. No horseshoes. Mortimer had even forgotten to bring a ball. I skipped pebbles for a while until Mortimer said, "Let's go for a walk."

Going for a walk with Mort isn't my idea of the way to spend an interesting day, but there wasn't much help for it. Mom and the senior Snaffles were discussing the political situation and it looked as though they might go on for hours. I shrugged and followed Mort up the hill.

"Take Petey," my mother called, but for some reason Petey didn't seem to want to leave. Maybe the political situation interests him more than it does me.

Mort headed for the barn. It was a ramshackle old affair, with a cupola on top and a sheep shed off to one side, but it looked as though it might be fun to explore. With anybody, that is, but Mortimer. Still, you have to make do with what you have at hand. I said, "Let's go inside, shall we?"

Mortimer was for it. We left the door partway open, and there was light from the windows that showed up the stanchions for cattle and the horse stalls and all. There was a hayloft up top, and we climbed to that. From the window you could see out all over Ivy Hill. "Not bad," I said.

But Mort didn't seem interested. He was fidgeting around with one hand in his pocket and first thing I knew he hauled out a pack of cigarettes and said, "Have one?" Just like that. Mortimer Augustus Snaffle III!

"Who, me?" Mort knows that none of the boys in our crowd smoke. Who wants to ruin his lungs?

He got the idea and shrugged. "Mind if I do?" He reached down with his mouth and came up with a cigarette, like the hard-boiled guys do in the movies. He lighted it and started to smoke.

If this was a gag meant to impress me, I didn't react. You can't tell a guy Mort's age he's acting like a dummy without asking for a fight, and Mortimer is three inches taller than me and has gained a lot of weight all of a sudden. Besides, I had a feeling that my mother had been tried far enough, so far as this picnic was concerned. I moseyed around the loft, waiting for him to finish, and he leaned against the window jamb, inhaling and exhaling and pretending to enjoy the whole thing when actually he was half choking.

I was getting more fed up by the minute. Through a broken pane in the grimy window I could see signs of activity down by the creek. Mom was laying a big white cloth and Mr. Snaffle must have been tinkering with the charcoal grill, because a thin line of smoke was curling upward.

"It looks like we eat soon," I mentioned.

The words were no sooner out of my mouth than I heard Mr. Snaffle give an angry shout. Then Mrs. Snaffle screamed, and Petey came galloping right across the white picnic cloth and up the hill toward the barn.

"Petey! Come back!"

"Er-nie!" That was Mom. "Ernie, get him. Get him, Ernie!"

"Petey! Petey!"

In a second all three of the grown-ups were after my dog, yelling at the top of their lungs. They all sounded mad as anything, and as Petey got closer I could see the reason. He had something in his mouth.

There was no question in my mind about what it was. I know Petey. He is very, very fond of hamburg.

Now while hamburg, in my mind, shouldn't be spoken of in the same breath with sirloin, on a picnic it is better than no meat at all. And it looked as though no meat was what we were going to have, unless I could do something about it. I skidded down the ladder and landed almost on top of Petey himself.

"Hey!" I shouted as I came.

Petey was so surprised by this bomb from above that he dropped the package of meat.

In no time at all everybody was gathered around us —Mr. and Mrs. Snaffle, my mother, and Mortimer. "Everything's under control," I said calmly. "Here's the hamburg." I dusted it off and held it out to Mr. Snaffle before he could say, "That dog!"

Mom just looked from Petey to me and set her lips.

We all walked back to the picnic ground, Mr. Snaffle limping a little because he had turned his ankle in a muskrat hole on the way up from the stream. "I can feel it swelling," he complained. He eased himself down onto the ground near the charcoal grill and took off his shoe. "There, that's better," he said.

The hamburgers tasted good when they were done.

Mom's sandwiches and deviled eggs did too. When it comes to food there's something to be said for a picnic, even a picnic with the Snaffles. By the time we were finished we were all so full we just sat and looked at one another. That is, everybody else looked at one another. I got tired of Snaffle faces, so I looked up at the barn . . .

I couldn't believe my eyes!

Out of the broken pane in the loft window was coming a thin spiral of smoke!

First I thought I was imagining things. I'd had fire on my mind for so long it was making me balmy. But a light breeze was beginning to whip the tops of the trees and it fanned the smoke a bit. I sniffed. It was real all right. And here I was, at the wrong end of a fire!

"Lookit!" I said.

Mr. Snaffle looked. Mrs. Snaffle looked. Mom looked. And Mortimer looked too, turning a little green in the process. He was remembering something, and I knew what it was—that cigarette.

In an instant he was on his feet, running toward the barn. His dad got up, too, and started to follow him, before he remembered his ankle. He yelped once and sank back with a groan.

I didn't move. I was doing some fancy thinking. Already a bright tongue of flame was licking along the loft windowsill. Obviously, Mort and I, with a pail or two of water from the brook, weren't going to save that barn. And if it wasn't saved, and the fire-insurance company investigated, who do you think the fire would be blamed on?

Mortimer?

Not on your life! Mort would manage to weasel out of it and shift the blame to Petey. He'd have a point, because if Petey hadn't stolen that hamburg, Mort would never have dropped his cigarette without stamping on the butt.

Once I reached this conclusion, I acted fast. I started running away from the fire and out toward the main road as fast as I could go. The first car by gave me a lift and we stopped at the nearest house likely to have a telephone. As luck would have it, nobody was home, so instead of wasting still more time, the guy who had picked me up made a beeline for the fire-house. I shouted the news as I ran inside and was the first man to reach the engine.

We whipped out to the Clarke place on the double, picking up other volunteers along the way, and by the time we arrived the fire was really raging, making something worth spraying water on.

Except there was no source of water, back in the Clarke woods. You couldn't fill a big bucket, let alone a fire hose, from that piddling little brook. But modern fire-fighting equipment is neat. Our truck had a chemical tank aboard, and pressure hoses, and all that stuff. Let me tell you, things got really exciting for the next half hour!

We saved the barn, too—the lower part of it, that is. Of course, what's left is mostly stone. After it was all over and Ken found out that this was the place we had been picnicking, he looked at me very suspiciously.

"Come clean, Ernie. Did you start that fire?" he asked.

"No. Petey did," I answered before I thought. But

113

Ken's a good friend of mine. He won't give Petey away.

And as for Mortimer, I'll bet he'll lay off smoking for a long, long time. Some people have to learn sense the hard way!

CHAPTER TEN

Petey Performs

IT WAS RIGHT AFTER the fire in the barn that Mort began giving me a really hard time. He resented the fact that I had something on him and took every opportunity to make fun of Petey. Through Petey, naturally, he got to me.

Six months before, I would have knocked him down for saying the things he did, but now that Mortimer is three inches taller and ten pounds heavier than I am, this would be asking for bad trouble. Still, a man of honor can take just so much.

We were walking back from a softball game one morning—Ken, Buzz, Mortimer, and me—when Petey spotted us at the end of Persimmon Lane and came bounding down the road to greet us, grinning like a great big pup.

"Hyah, Petey!" I said.

"Hyah, Petey!" said Buzz and Ken.

"Boy, he's a bruiser to be such a lily-livered numb-skull," said Mortimer, just like that, with no excuse at all.

I wanted to sock him right then and there, but I had better sense. "See here," I said, keeping my temper, "just because Petey isn't a guard dog is no reason for slander."

"He got turned down, didn't he? Being gun-shy is a physical disability, just like being lame in one leg."

What a thing to say! If Buzz and Ken hadn't grabbed me by the arms, I'd have torn that Snaffle sniffer limb from limb. I'd have—

But I didn't. I just spluttered, in a voice that squeaked a bit because it's changing. "Mortimer Snaffle, I'll make you eat those words!"

After he had walked on down the street, with a sneer on his face so big I could almost see it from behind, Ken and Buzz unhanded me and we all sat down on my front steps.

"How?" asked Ken.

"How what?"

"How are you going to make him eat those words?"

"Well," I started, puffing out my chest. Then I deflated like a pricked balloon and admitted, "I don't know."

Buzz got up and swung his baseball bat back and forth, as though it might be useful as a weapon. Then he heard the noon whistle. "Coming along, Ken? If you get any good ideas, Ernie, give us a call. We'll do anything we can to help."

They left me sitting there, with Petey towering alongside, and I kept muttering, "The nerve of that pipsqueak!" to myself. The trouble was I'd be bound to lose if I tried to cream him. Those three inches and ten pounds couldn't be ignored.

A few minutes later a green station wagon that was idling past stopped right in front of our house. A middle-aged, puffy-faced man with a bald head stuck his neck out of the window and said, of all things, "Hello, little boy."

First Petey gets insulted, then me. I stared right back at the man and said, "Hi!" very sourly. Next I asked, so he'd catch on, "Were you talking to *me?*"

"That your dog?"

"Yeah," I replied in a what's-it-to-you tone of voice.

The man pulled the car over to the side of the road, shifted to "park," and climbed out. Petey, the dope, stood up and wagged his tail.

This seemed to please the puffy stranger. He said, "Here, fellow!" and clicked his fingers the way people do when they don't understand dogs. Petey marched down the walk and posed.

"A magnificent specimen," the man murmured, walking around Petey fearlessly and considering him from every angle. "A truly magnificent specimen!"

"He's not for sale," I said. Nevertheless, I was pleased to have Petey appreciated by a guy three times as old as Mortimer Snaffle.

"Ho!" boomed the fat man. "I wasn't thinking of buying him. I was just looking him over. He's very photogenic, you know."

"Very *what?*" I didn't quite catch the word, and my fists clenched automatically. I wasn't going to let Petey be called names twice in one day.

"Photogenic. You know—he'd take a good picture."

I relaxed. "Yeah, he does. I've got some swell snapshots."

"Has he ever posed commercially?"

I shook my head.

"Tell you what I'd like to do," the man said. "I'd like to take this dog of yours in to our Boston studio and see how he'd behave under lights."

When I looked puzzled he explained that he wanted to take pictures of Petey for possible use in advertising Peppy Pup Dog Food. Digging around in his pants pocket, he came up with a business card, which he handed to me. "There's not a great deal of money in it, Junior, but your trip to town would be worth ten bucks or so."

"How would we get there?" I asked.

"Oh, I'd come pick you up," the man replied nonchalantly. He glanced at his watch. "I've got to leave now, but give me your name and phone number and I'll give you a ring in a couple of days. O.K.?"

"O.K.," I said, standing there with the card in my hand as he climbed back into his car and rolled away. "Benjamin Steen," it read. "Harold I. Stretch and Sons, Advertising."

"Who was that?" Mom asked, coming to the door to call me for lunch.

"Some guy from an advertising agency in town. He may want to take Petey's picture."

"Well, that would be nice," said my mother.

"I'll bet I never hear from the guy," I said pessimistically. Whenever there's money involved in a deal, I seem to be the unlucky type.

Still, the interview gave me a lift. The mere possibility of Petey's picture appearing in a newspaper or magazine seemed to clear his reputation. Five minutes later I found myself telling Mom all about Mortimer Snaffle's habit of bugging me in front of Ken and Buzz.

To my surprise, this seemed to incense my mother as much as it did me. "Every boy, at least once in his lifetime, runs afoul of a bully," she said. "Mortimer's sudden growth spurt has given him the nerve to pick on you, but you mustn't allow it to go on, Ernie. You'll have to stand up to him, even if you get hurt."

"You mean—fight? I'd be creamed."

"I can't help it," said Mom, who is usually so mild and even-tempered. "It's the only way."

Well, you could have knocked me over with a feather, which was just what Mortimer would undoubtedly do if I got up the courage to pick a scrap. My front teeth aren't very pretty but I've become used to them, and since I didn't want to have them knocked out, I decided to avoid him for the next few days.

This wasn't easy to do, since he lived only three doors down the street, but I managed. And by hanging around the house so much I happened to be home when Mr. Steen phoned.

"How about letting me pick up you and your dog about two o'clock tomorrow afternoon?" he suggested.

"O. K.," I answered. "O. K. Fine!"

Mom thought Petey smelled a little "doggy," so the next morning I gave him a bath. I have learned from experience that unless I have help, the only sensible way to give Petey a bath is to tie him with a piece of clothesline to the apple tree at the foot of the driveway between our house and Browns', then get into swimming trunks and hitch up the garden hose. After I get Petey thoroughly wet, I always lather him with flea soap. Petey sort of enjoys this, and when I get his back finished he's apt to lie down and put all four paws in the air so I can do his stomach. Well, just about the time Petey rolled on his back, who should come along the street but Mortimer Snaffle.

"Itsy-bitsy Petesy having his bath?" he yelled in a voice that was definitely nasty. "Take good care of him, Ernie! He might catch cold!"

I thought the best thing to do was to ignore him, but I hadn't forgotten Mom's advice. I decided that as soon as we got this photography business over with I'd go to work in earnest on Mortimer.

Mr. Steen arrived on time and Petey and I were completely ready, besides which we even smelled good. This seemed to please Mr. Steen, who hustled us into his car and zipped right into town. We parked about a block from a tall office building, and I fastened on Petey's rope and coaxed him out of the car. Petey is not used to city noises, and he would have preferred to stay right where he was.

It took a little doing to get Petey into the elevator in the lobby of the building, and we collected quite a crowd. But we finally got him to Mr. Steen's studio, where a lot of big lights were rigged up, with cords that lay all over the floor. Mr. Steen began to arrange Petey behind a package of Peppy Pup Dog Food while I stood in the background, looking on.

First he had Petey stand up, and I thought he looked very handsome, but Mr. Steen said he made the dog-food package look too small. "The idea," he explained, "is to show what a husky animal Peppy Pup can produce. But at the same time the product's got to be played up. That makes it difficult."

I could see that made it difficult. Petey was asked to sit down, lie down, and curl up. The lights were hot, in spite of air conditioning. Before very long both Petey and Mr. Steen were in a lather. I will say, however, that Petey behaved to perfection. He likes to be the center of attention.

Finally Mr. Steen sat right down in the middle of the floor and tore his hair. "It won't work!" he bawled. "It simply won't suit the client. He's a very fussy sort."

I didn't know anything about the client, but I could see that things weren't exactly going our way. "You mean we—I mean, Petey, doesn't get paid?"

Mr. Steen looked at me and said, "There's nothing in the budget for failures."

First Petey gets called a lily-livered numbskull and now he gets called a failure! I looked at Petey and gritted my teeth. "He could hold the package in his mouth," I suggested.

Mr. Steen was on his feet in a fat man's flash. "Son," he shouted, "I think you've got it!"

"Do I get a bonus?" I murmured, but he pretended not to hear me, or maybe he was just very busy pushing the package of dog food between Petey's teeth.

"Hold it, Petey," I commanded.

Petey held it. He looked great, but he must have felt foolish, because just as Mr. Steen clicked the camera Petey gave me that simpleminded grin he sometimes pulls.

Several shots were taken after that, but the first one —the grinny one—was the picture they used. A proof of it came out to the house a few days later, along with a note saying that the model's fee would follow shortly, along with a "release" for Mom to sign, stating that she didn't object to Petey's picture appearing in advertising.

I rushed right over to show Ken and Buzz the picture of Petey, because I thought he looked so great.

"Boy," said Buzz appreciatively. "You've got something there! Wait until Mort sees that in a magazine."

"He'll turn green with jealousy," Ken agreed. "Beau will have to take a back seat at last."

"I'd like to see his face when he comes across it," Buzz added. "Maybe they'll publish Petey's picture in a Boston newspaper. Wouldn't that be cool?"

Two weeks later, after I'd received a check for not ten, but fifteen dollars, that is precisely what happened. Petey's picture appeared in a half-page full-color ad in the Boston *Globe.* Mortimer Snaffle couldn't miss it, because it was right opposite the funnies. Boy, was I proud!

I chased over to Ken's with the good news and the torn-out page. Petey was with me, of course. Just as I got there Mortimer passed on his bike, yelling something insulting, as usual. For the first time I didn't feel scared. In fact, I yelled right back.

Apparently this was the reaction he had been waiting for. While Buzz and Ken watched, he circled around Petey and me, bringing the bike closer and closer and calling us dirty names. He really is a bully, just like Mom said.

I was desperate.

There was a stick lying in the road. Suddenly I bent down and picked it up. Mortimer thought I was going to try to hit him and it made him laugh. Instead I jammed the stick between the spokes of his front wheel and Mortimer Snaffle shot over the handlebars and landed with a crack on the macadam road.

I was on him in a flash, and since the breath was knocked out of him, the rest was easy. I socked him a couple of times, then bloodied his nose for good measure. Finally I sat on his chest with my knees pinching his ribs and dictated a statement for Mortimer to sign. This read, "Petey Bodman is not a lily-livered numbskull." Ken handed it to me and I rolled it up in a ball.

"Now eat it!" I ordered.

He would have, too, if Mrs. Snaffle hadn't happened to come by at that moment and rescued her darling boy. As it is, I've got it tucked away behind the socks in my top bureau drawer, in case there should be a next time.

CHAPTER ELEVEN

Down Under
or Up Front?

UNCLE ZACH'S LETTER came as a bolt from the
blue Pacific. Not that we weren't used to hearing from
him. We usually got a long letter every month or so,
but this one was different.

It arrived on a Saturday morning while Mom was
vacuuming the dust babies under my maple bed. She
stopped working to tear open the envelope and unfold
the single sheet. An oblong of paper drifted to the
floor, and I picked it up in a hurry, because anybody
could see that it was a check. We don't get too many
checks in our house, and this one was a whopper.

"Golly!" I breathed, blinking. "A thousand dollars!"

Mom held out her hand, quite unperturbed. "Give
it to me, Ernie, and stop teasing."

She glanced at the check and sank down onto the
bed as if she had been struck. "What? Has Zach
taken leave of his senses?"

"Maybe the letter will explain," I suggested helpfully.

Surprise was piled upon surprise, because Uncle
Zach was inviting us to pack up and fly out to Australia
within the next month. "You can rent the house in Ivy

Hill for a year," he proposed, "and if you don't like it here, you can pack up and go home. But it's a great country, the bee business is booming, the people are friendly, and I think you'll love it. At least give it a try!"

Mom read the letter aloud with mounting excitement. She has always had an urge to travel, and on winter nights she's apt to sit poring over the *National Geographic*, but New York City is the farthest away from New England she has ever been.

Her eyes were shining when she looked up at me. "What an adventure it would be for us, Ernie! The other side of the world. Down Under! Ten thousand miles away."

A shiver of anticipation chased up my spine, because I could see Mom was sold. But my heart gave a dull thud. "What about Petey?" I asked. "Is he invited too?"

For the moment my mother had forgotten all about Petey. She came back to reality with a jerk that made her wince. "Petey *is* a complication," she admitted. "Maybe Ken or Buzz would take care of him. Or we might put him in a kennel. Or even rent him along with the house."

None of these suggestions made any sense, as my mother knew perfectly well. Ken and Buzz both have dogs of their own, three hundred and fifty-two days of kennel care for a Great Dane would cost more than our air fare, and people don't rent dogs that eat as much as Petey does unless they're slightly out of their heads. Mom was grasping at straws, because the idea of Australia gripped her. I could see now that for several months Uncle Zach had been making a soft sell.

126

Talking Australia up in all those letters. Telling Mom how comparatively cheap food was, writing about a kid my age with a pet kangaroo, putting in rave notices about the countryside and the lack of smog and all that. Now, as a clincher, he said Mom was really needed to give a hand in the business and to run the house. If there is anything Mom likes, it's to be needed, even ten thousand miles away.

For the rest of the day she had a strange expression in her eyes when she looked at Petey. It was as though she'd like to give him a drink like the one Alice in Wonderland took that made her shrink. "If only he were a toy poodle," she complained. "I don't know why Zach had to give you such a *big* dog! It's all his fault, actually."

"There's no use talking that way," I said staunchly. "Petey is here to stay."

Stay is a word that Petey understands. He looked at me approvingly and sat down, while Mom paced back and forth across the living room like an animal in a cage. It was plain to see she wanted out.

Sunday she spent the morning paying bills and the afternoon leafing through old copies of the *National Geographic*. She showed me pictures of koala bears and aborigines and herds of sheep and the Sydney Zoo, but nothing made Petey grow any smaller. He still took up nearly half the living room rug.

On Monday morning my mother got dressed for town and announced that she was going to Boston to talk to some airline people. She wasn't giving up Australia without a struggle, and she told me that I was to cut Petey down to half rations. "He's getting entirely too fat," she said.

127

"Petey is not fat. He's just big," I told her.

"Well, he's got to reduce," Mom retorted. Without any further explanation, she picked up her purse and marched off.

I had a sneaking suspicion that she was visiting the airlines personally in order to find out what the rules and regulations were about taking a Great Dane along. I looked at Petey dubiously and hoped he'd be overweight, which would squash the whole idea. Although Petey is enormous, he has a delicate and fearful disposition and needs constant reassurance from Mom or me. I couldn't visualize Petey confined to a cage in a dark freight compartment down under the passenger cabin of an airplane. He might think the roar of the engines was thunder. He'd go berserk! He might even have a brain hemorrhage. Mom might as well give up, I decided, and I put all thoughts of going to Australia out of my mind. Leaving Petey behind was unthinkable and taking him along just wouldn't work.

My mother, however, is a persistent woman. She came home from Boston armed with all sorts of facts and figures about dogs accompanying passengers in airplanes.

"Only dogs weighing eleven pounds or less are allowed to fly with their owners," she said. "You can see why. Big dogs can't sit in people's laps."

There was no argument to the fact that Petey couldn't sit in my lap. He'd squash me.

"We'd have to have a crate made," Mom continued. "The cargo holds are pressurized and heated, they tell me. He'd be quite all right."

"He'd die of fright," I said stubbornly.

"Not if he was tranquilized."

128

"Suppose we flew through a thunderstorm?"

"The freight compartments are as soundproof as the cabin," replied my mother. She had done her research thoroughly and I began to feel alarmed.

"It would be positively inhuman," I muttered. "You know it, Mom!"

"Mother," she corrected me from force of habit. "The real problem is the expense, because they charge for dogs by the pound, like excess baggage. Still, if your Uncle Zach is doing so well with his business, he may be willing to foot the bill. I'm going to write to him at once and find out."

I heaved a sigh of relief, because I remembered Uncle Zach as being pretty thrifty. I couldn't see him ponying up several hundred dollars extra to bring Petey along unless he could put him to work. And I don't think Petey would ever get to understand bees, much less learn to herd sheep. Besides, he might not like mutton, and I understand that in Australia people and dogs don't eat much beef. The more I thought about this wild scheme of flying halfway across the world with a Great Dane in tow, the sillier I thought it was.

Sure that Uncle Zach would think it was just as foolish as I did, I saw no real reason to worry. I told Ken and Buzz about Uncle Zach's letter because it made a good story, and because I was sure that they would agree with me. Instead, their eyes popped with envy. "You mean you'd actually turn down a chance to go to Australia because of a dog?" Ken asked.

"Petey's no ordinary dog. He's a member of our family." I was insulted and I showed it.

Buzz was more understanding. "I read a newspaper

piece about a lion that died of fright when he was being flown from East Africa to London," he said helpfully.

My stomach gave a flip, and I looked at Ken angrily. "You see?"

But Ken did not see. He was like my mother, travel-crazy, and he just couldn't understand why Petey should have priority over a trip to such a far-off place. "You'd have a chance to go to Honolulu on the way," he said, "and maybe even to Fiji or to New Zealand. Gosh, and you'd fly right over all those islands in the South Seas."

"Those big jets fly so high you'd never see the islands," Buzz said sensibly, while I was thinking of Petey, tucked away all by himself in the freight compartment, scared to death.

A week passed, while I tried to put the whole thing out of my mind and Ken continued to regard me enviously. Mom, in the meantime, was doing homework on Australia and coming up with some curious facts. "They eat hot meat pies the way we eat hamburgers," she said as if this was some big deal.

"Who likes meat pies?" I muttered.

Mom tried again. "Myna birds are very common. They can be trained to talk, like parrots. Isn't that interesting?"

"They also have furry tarantulas," I told her, to show I knew something about Australia too.

Mom hates spiders, but she didn't turn a hair. "They're not poisonous in Australia," she murmured. "They just kill flies."

It takes a while to get a letter to and from Australia, even longer than it takes to get one to Boston, so Mom had plenty of time to work on me and to try to whip up my enthusiasm, which was nil. She kept reminding me that Uncle Zach had bought a former sheep ranch of a thousand acres outside of Melbourne.

"A thousand acres is a lot of land," she said. "Petey would have plenty of room to run."

This really hit me, because a month ago the developers moved into the field at the bottom of the hill. Where our truck gardens were last summer, houses are going up. The brook has just about disappeared, and there's nowhere at all for Petey to get any real exercise.

Even so, the more I thought about it, the less I wanted to go to Australia. I had finally grown accustomed to Ivy Hill after the move from the farm, and the thought of leaving Buzz and Ken and the rest of the kids for a whole year made me feel sick inside. There was no use hoping that things would be the same when I got back, because they wouldn't be. They just never are! I wouldn't even consider the thought that Mom might decide to stay in Australia forever. She belongs in New England, the same way I do. This travel bug of hers was for the birds.

Never before had home seemed so cozy. Until now I'd never realized what swell guys my friends were. Even Mortimer Snaffle seemed to be improving, and I actually grinned at Bunny Jameson when I passed him on the street. Everybody and everything about Ivy Hill seemed better than ever before.

"Taking Petey to Australia is plain kooky," I told Mom, without saying a word about my own feelings. "He'd be like that lion. He wouldn't survive."

"Nonsense," said my mother.

"How would *you* like to ride in a luggage compartment?"

"That isn't the question." But Mom began looking at Petey in a considering sort of way. "Petey's big but he is quiet," she said after a few minutes. "We could ask for a front seat in the tourist section, where there is extra leg room. He could sit between us, curled up, and nobody would even know he was there. He's certainly a lot less apt to create a disturbance than most babies I've seen."

This was just a ploy to mollify me, as I knew perfectly well. Anyway, I didn't believe for a minute that Uncle Zach would cough up Petey's fare.

That's where I was wrong. In less than two weeks a delighted reply came from Uncle Zach, along with another big fat check that would take care of Petey. Mom was thrilled. The very next day she went into Boston again and made the rounds of the airlines, and after hours spent cooling her heels in the anterooms of various managers, she had a real break.

One guy admitted a weakness for Great Danes. He owned one himself, and agreed that they were the most good-natured of all breeds. So, after contacting his head office, he told Mom the decision was up to the captain, but if he agreed, the three of us could ride in the first seat in the tourist section. What would happen from San Francisco on he couldn't guarantee, but Mom was willing to trust to luck.

She promised to get a prescription for tranquilizers from the vet. She promised to starve Petey for the day before takeoff. She promised that he was extremely well behaved and more gentle than any lamb she had ever known, which was the truth.

Even so, I had reservations. When the house was put up for rent, I had a sinking feeling, and when a carpenter came and started to make a crate big enough to hold Petey, I blew my top. "What's this thing for?" I yelled.

"It's just a safeguard," Mom said calmly.

"A safeguard for what? You know he hates cages!"

"I had to promise the airline company," Mom replied. She was certainly in a promising mood.

She even promised me I'd love Australia, although of course I realized she didn't know what she was talking about. She told me I was a very lucky boy to be able to take Petey, as though there was any question of leaving him behind!

She promised Petey he was lucky, too, that he'd adjust very quickly. That was wishful thinking, of course. "Imagine having a thousand acres to romp in!" she cried as she rubbed his muzzle. Although she was talking to Petey, she was glancing up sideways at me.

Suddenly, everything began to speed up. The first family that came to see the house rented it, furnished, and Mom began to pack all her valuables and store them away in the attic. Who carried the boxes upstairs? Guess.

Ken and Buzz came over almost every afternoon. They weren't much help but they were company, and Petey, who suspected that something was up, had taken to spending his days as far away from this hive of activity as he could get.

When the suitcases finally came out he got the shivers. You can't fool Petey. He *knows!* The trouble was I couldn't explain that he was going with us. Or maybe if I had, the shakes would have been even

133

worse. Already he was a wreck from the veterinarian's house visit, when he submitted to the necessary shots only after being fed a massive dose of tranqilizers.

It seemed crazy to be packing all our winter clothes at the beginning of summer, but Mom explained that it would be winter when we got to Australia, and this didn't make me any more optimistic about the trip. "Though it never gets very cold," she said soothingly, "and I understand that there are more than seven hours of sunlight a day, on the average."

"On the average! The tourist boards always get you with that."

Mom stopped wrapping her flat silver in flannel cases and said, "Will you please stop being difficult?"

"It's not me," I muttered unhappily. "It's Petey who's going to be difficult. Just you wait!"

My mother is not easily intimidated, especially by her own son. Come hell or high water, we were going to Australia, and Petey and I could like it or lump it.

On the day before we were to leave, the fact that we would be away for a whole year, at least, really got to me. I couldn't say good-by to Ken and Buzz, who came over with bon voyage presents. We just kidded around and I tried not to think that they'd be sophomores in high school by the time I got back. I kept wondering what the Aussie kids would be like. They probably talked Cockney and it would be hard to understand them. I'd already heard one on television. He kept calling himself "Austrine." Besides, they'd play cricket instead of baseball, and it was a game I knew less than nothing about. The whole prospect was depressing, if you asked me.

I'll admit, though, that if I hadn't been worrying

about Petey, I'd have been getting a little excited about going to the ends of the earth. Me, Ernie Bodman. Imagine! Flying in an airplane for ten thousand miles.

But when I'd look at that innocent dog lying out front with his rear end up on the top step and his big paws on the sidewalk, my stomach would flip over again. I kept hoping—I actually prayed!—that Captain Number 1 would be understanding. I couldn't think far enough ahead to imagine Captain Number 2.

We left Ivy Hill in Mr. Brown's Volkswagen bus at seven o'clock in the morning—my mother, Petey, and I. We would have taken a taxi except for the crate. Even in the Volkswagen bus, with all our luggage, it was a tight squeeze.

Mom was effusive when she said thank you and good-by to our next-door neighbor in front of the airline terminal. She even kissed him on the cheek. I was so busy trying to explain to the porters that Petey wouldn't bite that I never even saw Mr. Brown drive off.

The crate took up an entire luggage cart. The porter led Petey and me around back like second-class citizens while Mom checked in and all that stuff. It was going to be a hot day. Already Petey was panting and shivering, both at the same time. The porter parked us by the motorized luggage van, and looked from Petey to the crate. "You better get that animal in there pretty fast," he said, then hurried back to get his tip from Mom.

It's a strange feeling, being stranded on the tarmac of a big airport like Logan, with other passengers inside a wall of windows looking out at you. Petey and I were both so nervous we twitched, and I wondered why they even let us stay there, on the wrong side of the No ADMITTANCE sign. Half an hour passed—slowly—and I began to scan the windows looking for Mom. My throat felt tight and my mouth was dry. I'd have given anything for a Coke.

Each passing minute made me more worried and fidgety. If the plane was crowded, they'd never let Petey ride up front with us, never! I began to feel that Mom had tricked me, that she herself hadn't really believed that the captain would allow such a thing.

The only good thing about the long wait was that Petey's tranquilizer began to work. He lay down, put his head on his paws, and went to sleep, as if jets weren't roaring around in all directions and that crate with the door ajar wasn't sitting within a foot of him.

Activity began to pick up. A jeep pulled away from the big jet that loomed almost over our heads and men in mechanics uniforms hurried up and down the outside steps that led into the vestibule with the bellows arrangement clamped onto the plane's front door. The luggage van was rolled away and a guy shouted over his shoulder to me, "I'll be back in a sec for your dog."

My heart went plunk, right down to the soles of my loafers, because I knew he expected the dog to be in the crate. I looked up at the staring windows frantically.

Then a miracle happened. The door at the top of the outside steps opened, and a man in a blue uniform with wings on his chest and four stripes on his sleeves came running down the stairs two at a time, while Mom stood at the top beckoning and grinning from ear to ear. In two shakes Petey and I were ushered upstairs and whisked into the tourist section of the plane ahead of all the other passengers. The stewardesses were laughing and smiling, the captain was patting Petey on the head, and Mom was almost weeping from relief. Everything was just great. Petey slept by the forward partition while Mom and I enjoyed the movie.

The trouble began at San Francisco! There Petey stumbled down the plane steps groggily, because of the pill, and began sniffing around for a nonexistent patch of grass. Suddenly our arrangement in the tourist section was ripped apart by an indignant airport official.

"What is this?" the man shouted. "A dog?"

I bit back the possible retorts. "His name is Petey," I told him.

"Where's his cage? He should be in his cage!"

I had to admit that the crate was in the belly of the airplane. "But he's traveling tourist class."

"We'll get it out!" the official shouted, paying no attention to my explanation. He raced off to order the big crate lowered immediately to the ground. Other passengers had to wait for their luggage, but Petey got his on the double. "Put him in there," growled the uniformed man. "Now!"

I looked appealingly at Mom, but she shrugged and spread her hands, eyeing the official dubiously. The friendly captain had vanished, and our cause looked hopeless.

Petey, however, was so tranquil that he didn't object to entering the crate at all. He stepped inside with a rather drunken lurch, then turned around carefully, wincing only when the door was slammed in his face.

I scratched his muzzle through the wire mesh, and

137

he wagged his tail, which protruded from the opposite end. Mom hurried off to try to talk some sense into the San Francisco people, but I stayed with Petey while the rest of the luggage was unloaded and the cleanup crew went aboard the plane. A fuel-oil truck arrived, a caterer's van came and went, but Mom didn't reappear. I stood by helplessly watching the ground crew stow away several cartfuls of baggage and heave three sacks of mail aboard.

At last it was definitely Petey's turn. With Mom somewhere inside that huge, unfriendly airport, I had to watch four hefty young men in jump suits jockey Petey's crate into the maw of the plane.

Petey was so dazed and sedated that he didn't even bark in protest, but a small black poodle in a pint-sized carrier was raising a terrible row. The only thing I could hope was that maybe they'd keep each other company. Never have I felt so low and miserable about Australia—or anything else.

A guy in a different kind of uniform came up and shooed me inside the terminal building, asking how I got out there anyway. Mom showed up again, looking more discouraged than ever, and we were hustled back to our old seats by a new group of stewardesses.

"Never mind, Ernie." Mom patted my hand. "He'll be all right." She tried to sound convincing, but I could tell she was almost as concerned as I was.

The hop to Honolulu was a long one. I couldn't eat the meal that was served, although it smelled good, because my stomach kept turning over. People began to take catnaps, and even my mother closed her eyes and dozed, but I couldn't sleep for thinking about Petey, down in that dark hole somewhere below, with only that yappy black poodle for company. I imagined how he must have felt when we taxied down the runway and raced along the takeoff strip. I was with him in spirit as we rose into the air and climbed to reach the altitude at which we were now flying. If Petey didn't have a nervous breakdown after this, I'd be surprised.

Actually, if it was only a nervous breakdown, he'd be lucky. The palms of my hands turned clammy when I thought about that lion Buzz had told me about. If anything happened to Petey, I'd sue the airline for a million dollars, that's what I'd do! Making a sensitive dog like him ride in the luggage compartment! It would serve them right if he collapsed and—

"Ernie?" Mom's voice was close to my left ear.

"H'm?"

"You did remember to give Petey another tranquilizer, didn't you?"

No, I hadn't remembered. I hadn't even thought

139

about it while I stood there beside his crate. He was so doped up already that the idea that the tranquilizer might wear off before we got to Honolulu had never entered my mind.

This was the last straw—Petey down there gradually awakening to a terror that might make him go berserk. I could see him thrashing against the sides of the crate, cut and bleeding, abandoned by his family, whom he'd never be able to trust again.

"How many more hours?" I croaked.

"About two, I think," Mom replied gently.

They were the worst two hours I have ever spent. For a good deal of the time I felt as though I *was* Petey. I suffered as a dog must suffer when he is deserted and alone and afraid. I vowed that if I ever got him out of that hold alive, I'd stay in Hawaii for the rest of my life, if necessary, before I'd let them do such a thing again.

My mother didn't say much, but she kept wringing her hands, so I knew she was worried too. When the seat-belt sign went on, finally, she breathed a long, tremulous sigh.

For me, the next ten minutes were sheer agony. Scenes from Petey's short but colorful life kept flashing before my eyes like pictures from a projector. Petey taking off after that cat at the baby parade. Petey going off to be a guard dog with a lei around his neck. Petey posing for Peppy Pup Dog Food and behaving beautifully. Petey curled up beside me on the living room rug, fast asleep and snoring. Trusting me. I could have bawled.

We were standing in the aisle while the plane was still moving, even though it's strictly forbidden. Mom was just as anxious as I was, and in spite of the glimpse we'd had of palm trees and tall buildings and blue water, neither of us was excited about landing in Honolulu. Petey was the only thing we cared about.

Since his crate had been the last thing to go into the hold, it was the first thing to come out, and the expression on the faces of the dark-skinned islanders who heaved and hauled the bulky contraption out into the daylight was something you'd have to have seen to believe.

Petey was no longer tranquil. He was standing up and barking like a banshee at all those strangers, who handled the cage as though they had a bull in a pen. It bumped when it hit the ground, and they backed away from it cautiously. Mom and I were standing as close as we were allowed, but Petey didn't see us until I started to jump up and down and call his name.

Then he turned his big, handsome head in our direction, and if a dog can smile, Petey smiled, in greeting and relief. An instant later there was a splintering sound, the door of the crate burst open, and he launched himself like a torpedo, almost knocking me over.

People scattered like a flock of pigeons. Women in muumuus—those long flowered Hawaiian dresses—picked up their skirts and ran. Men backed away hastily, fear in their eyes. But Mom and I fell to our knees and hugged Petey like a long-lost relative. We kept repeating his name, over and over, the way people do when they are overwhelmed.

Once he had made sure we were real and right there, Petey raised his head and sniffed. Then, in the distance, he saw a patch of green grass, which he needed as much as he needed our reassuring voices. He bounded toward it without a second's hesitation, cutting through the crowd like a scythe.

A flower seller dropped her armful of leis, a young woman screamed, an old lady raised her umbrella like a bludgeon, three men in uniform came running, and Mom and I gave chase. Not that we had to go far. The grass was all Petey wanted to reach, and he was occupied quite happily for the next few minutes. After all, it had been more than nine hours since we had left Boston.

When he came back to us I slipped on his rope and led him back toward the crate, just to confirm the fact that it was wrecked for good and all. From now on the captain would have to sing a different tune. You can't have a Great Dane bouncing around loose in a baggage compartment and there wasn't a prayer of getting that cage repaired in an hour.

There was a good deal of argument with the "powers that be," but in the end Petey won. Fortified with another tranquilizer, he came back to his old position between our knees, and several passengers who had grown accustomed to him on the first lap of our long journey stopped to pat his head.

From Honolulu to Fiji, Petey became the pet of the people in the tourist section, who were bored enough by then to welcome any diversion. As Ken had predicted, we were flying above the clouds, and there was nothing to see.

Mom, Petey, and I all had good long naps and we felt quite refreshed when we landed at Nandi on the Fiji island of Viti Levu. This was just as well, because again there was a change of captains. Number 4 was a beagle man who distrusted Great Danes and was determined to ground us until we could get the crate repaired.

"We've got every seat in the tourist section filled," the new captain told Mom, "and I'm not going to fly into Sydney with an elephant sitting in the aisle."

"He is large," Mom admitted with a winning smile, "but he's very well behaved."

By this time our third captain had been won over to our side. "He has certainly proved himself on the last leg of this trip," he said, thoughtfully. At last he asked his replacement, "How many first-class passengers do you have?"

By incredible good luck, only two first-class travelers had shown up, so the captain proposed that we be stowed away up there, where we couldn't possibly disturb anyone. Petey lay with his paws crossed and awaited the verdict with dignity. He could tell he was again the center of attention and seemed to be enjoying himself.

Seniority is something I don't understand too well, but Captain Number 3 won because of it, according to my mother. After a bit more conversation Captain Number 4 told us to wait until the other passengers got on, then to take seats up front.

There were no neighboring passengers to pet Petey, but there were two stewardesses with little to do except feed the three of us. Petey ate for several of the first-class "no-shows" who hadn't turned up. He was happily full of steaks when we began our descent into Sydney at the dawn of a new day.

I craned my neck to see past Mom, who had the window seat. There the city lay, below us, with a huge harbor spanned by the curve of a bridge, peninsulas like arms reaching out into the Pacific Ocean, skyscrapers, red-roofed houses, and trees, trees, trees. Petey yawned, sat up, and leaned against me, hard.

The pilot eased the big plane onto the runway with just a bit of a bump when we hit. Then the engines reversed with a noise like thunder and Petey quivered and tried to get up on my lap.

I pushed him back to the floor and ordered, "Sit!" while Mom took a long breath of relief. "He really has been a lamb," she said, now that the ordeal was over.

She sounded so calm as she fussed with her purse and pulled on her gloves that I was sort of irritated. "Gee, Mom, aren't you getting excited?" I asked as the wheels stopped turning.

"Mother," she corrected automatically.

Unexpectedly, I gathered courage. "Even Mortimer Snaffle calls his mother Mom," I told her. "From now on I'm going to call you Mom too, like the rest of the kids. One timid soul in this family is enough!"

DATE DUE

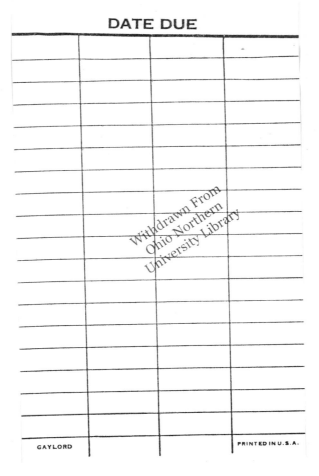

GAYLORD

PRINTED IN U.S.A.